Thorndike Press

9-8-01

2500

/

Where Tomorrow Waits

Also by Jane Peart
in Large Print:

The Westward Dreams Series
Runaway Heart
Promise of the Valley

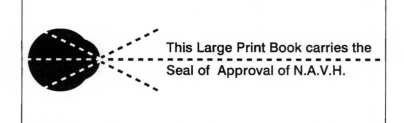

This Large Print Book carries the
Seal of Approval of N.A.V.H.

Westward Dreams Series

Book 3

Where Tomorrow Waits

Jane Peart

Thorndike Press • Waterville, Maine

Published in 2001 by arrangement with
Zondervan Publishing House.

Thorndike Press Large Print Christian Romance Series.

The tree indicium is a trademark of Thorndike Press.

The text of this Large Print edition is unabridged.
Other aspects of the book may vary from the original edition.

Set in 16 pt. Plantin by Rick Gundberg.

Printed in the United States on permanent paper.

Library of Congress Cataloging-in-Publication Data

Peart, Jane.
    Where tomorrow waits / Jane Peart.
        p.   cm. — (Westward dreams series ; bk. 3)
    ISBN 0-7862-3131-9 (lg. print : hc : alk. paper)
    1. Women pioneers — Fiction. 2. Large type books.
    I. Title.
    PS3566.E238 W48 2001
    813'.54—dc21   2001017121

PART 1

A Beckoning Dream

Chapter 1

"Have you ever thought much about California, Penny?"

"California?" Penny Sayres glanced at her sister-in-law, who was picking berries beside her. "You mean about the gold rush?"

"No, not exactly that" — Thea shook her head — "about the place itself?"

"Only what I've read — in school mostly. About Balboa discovering the Pacific Ocean. But I've forgotten most of it."

"I mean about going."

"Going? To *California?* You mean on a wagon train?"

"Well, yes, what it might be like —"

"Not really. . . ." Penny paused for a minute and stared at the slim, dark-haired young woman. "Why do you ask?"

Thea shrugged. "Just curious, I guess."

They went on picking berries for a few minutes more until Penny exclaimed, "Whew! It's sure hot for this late in September!" She whipped off her broad-brimmed straw hat and fanned herself to cool off. "Don't you think we have enough? Look." She held out her nearly full basket.

"I guess so." Thea sounded uncertain.

"Oh, I'm sure it is." Penny declared. "Anyway, I'm quitting. Come on, let's go on home and get us something cool to drink. We've picked plenty to make a nice batch of jam. Grams will be pleased as punch."

"Well, if you say so," Thea said even as she added a few more to her almost overflowing basket before setting it down. Then she turned to her plump, fifteen-month-old baby girl sitting on the blanket on the grass behind them. "Come on, Belinda, honey. Let's go see your daddy's grandma," she said, lifting her up into her arms.

"Grams is at Mrs. Bristow's. Quilting bee this afternoon," Penny told her, then made a silly face at her adored niece to try to make the baby smile. "Want me to carry her?"

"She's getting to be quite a load," Thea admitted.

"Here, you take my basket, and I'll give her a piggyback ride." The exchange was made, and Belinda crowed with delight as her aunt swung her around, settled her securely, and started jogging across the meadow toward the white frame farmhouse nestled under tall oak trees. When they reached the porch, Thea set down the baskets and took Belinda.

"Are you and Grams planning to go to the

church service this evening?" Thea asked.

"Oh, I don't think so," Penny replied. "Grams has had some trouble with her hip lately, and sitting too long on those hard benches gets to be a trial."

"It's not going to be just the ordinary Wednesday night prayer meeting. Tonight there's going to be a special speaker just come back from California. He's going to talk about the need for missionaries to the Indians in the western territories."

"So that's why you were asking me about California?" Penny smiled. "Frankly, I'm not much interested in that."

"Please, Penny, come with us!"

Penny, surprised at the urgency in her sister-in-law's voice, repeated, "Come with you?"

"Yes. I'd like you to hear what the man says too, because — Brad's all excited about it."

"Brad?" Penny said in surprise, knowing her brother had never been an overly zealous churchgoer. "Don't tell me *Brad's* interested in —" She halted, then asked in obvious disbelief, "You don't mean being *missionaries!"*

"Oh, my, *no!"* Thea shook her head. "It's the West he's interested in hearing about." Penny listened in amazement. Thea continued, "In fact, he's been reading all about it in all those pamphlets about how glorious everything is in the West."

"I've seen those posters in town, all about wanting emigrants to settle in the West. I've even read some of those frontier romances! But I don't believe any of it. Surely, Brad doesn't?"

"Oh, no! Not the romances!" Thea sounded shocked, then both of them laughed. "But he has read some of the written accounts about the real journey and about California. And he's interested in hearing the speaker tonight, because *he's* actually made the trip *twice.*"

They went inside. The house felt cool after the warmth of the afternoon and the exertion of rambling among the berry bushes.

"But what's that got to do with Brad wanting to go to *church* tonight?" Penny tossed her straw hat down and went over to the small mirror hung above the kitchen sink. She twisted her waist-length auburn braid into a knot on top of her head and secured it with a couple of hairpins she took from the pocket of her pinafore. "Brad's not exactly what you'd call a pillar of the church —" She halted suddenly then whirled around to face Thea "— that is, unless. . . ." She paused, then demanded, *"Unless* — he's not — Brad's *not* seriously thinking about going west? *Is* he?"

Thea's large eyes widened as she nodded

solemnly and answered, "Yes, I truly believe he is."

Penny frowned. Ever since the news of the discovery at Sutter's Fort had spread east and been written about in the newspapers, a lot of men had got "California fever." Even in the small rural community of Dunwoodie, Missouri, several men had left wives and families to go in search of gold. With a sinking heart Penny knew it was exactly the kind of thing that would spark her brother's impulsive nature. All those tall tales of instant riches would be just the thing to catch his imagination.

Warily Penny asked, "You don't mean Brad's thinking of *prospecting,* do you? Not *gold,* for heaven's sake?"

"No, not gold but land. You know if you homestead you can get acres and acres for practically nothing."

"But, Brad's doing so well. . . . You just got your house finished, and his carpentry business keeps him so busy. . . ."

"Yes, I know, but — he's been restless lately. He keeps talking about all the opportunities there are out west for a man. . . ." Thea shrugged. "*You* ought to know your brother, Penny."

Penny did indeed. From the time he was a little boy, Brad had a reckless streak and was easily bored. He was always looking for some

11

new excitement. After their parents' deaths and they'd come to live with Grams, Penny often used to wonder out loud if he was going to live long enough for Grams to raise him. He was always doing something dangerous, reckless, taking chances.

Thea smoothed Belinda's cheek. "She looks sleepy. I think I'll put her down on Grams' bed for a little nap, if that's all right. Then we can talk," Thea said over her shoulder as she carried the little girl, whose blond curly head was drooping onto her mother's shoulder, into the bedroom right off the kitchen. While Thea was out of the room, Penny squeezed lemons, stirred sugar into the juice, then mixed it with water from the kitchen pump. Frowning, she got down two tumblers from the whitewashed oak cabinet and put them on the table along with the pitcher and a plate of molasses cookies.

Why had Brad gotten all stirred up about going west? Just when everything was going so nicely! When he had fallen in love with the gentle Althea Rawlings and married her, both Penny and Grams had breathed a sigh of relief, thinking that he would settle down. But evidently he hadn't. After not quite three years of tranquil domesticity, Brad was thinking about going west?

"Her eyes closed the minute I put her

down," Thea announced as she came back into the kitchen. "Mmm, that looks lovely. I'm thirsty." She pulled out one of the ladder-back chairs and sat down at the table.

Thoughtfully Penny studied her brother's wife. Small, slender, delicate featured, Althea Rawlings hardly fit the picture of the stalwart pioneer woman taking over the reins of an ox-drawn covered wagon. Neither did she resemble one of those daredevil heroines of the dime novels Penny had sneaked upstairs to read under her covers as a girl. Actually they had been so preposterous she had ended up tossing them aside in disgust. She was sure the reality of the West was different from what either the novelists or the recruiters for wagon trains had written about it.

Thea took a long sip of lemonade. "The main reason Brad wants me to go tonight is to hear firsthand what it's like. Surely, a church speaker wouldn't make up something that wasn't true." Thea reached across the table and clutched Penny's hand. "That's why I want you and Grams to go and hear what this Brother Carmichael has to say. I'd like your opinion — you *and* Grams — your impressions. I trust Grams' judgment, and if she doesn't think it's a good idea . . . well, maybe she can persuade Brad."

Penny shook her head. "I don't know if

Grams has that kind of influence on him any-more. After all, Thea, he's a grown man —"
And an impulsive one, she added to herself. There was no use pointing *that* out to Thea, who adored her husband. His word was her command. If Brad wanted to go west. . . .

Thea's hand tightened on Penny's. "What I really want to know, Penny, *if* he *does* decide to go. . . ." She hesitated, then in a rush she asked, "Will *you* come with us?"

"Come with you to the *West? On a wagon train?*"

"Yes. That is, *if* Brad decides to go —"

"Oh, Thea, I don't think so. How could I leave Grams?" Penny withdrew her hand. "This is my home." She looked around at the rows of gleaming blue-and-white china on the oak hutch, the copper pans hung above the shiny black stove, the crisp, blue checkered curtains at the windows where the late after-noon sun streamed through the panes. "I've lived here all my life."

"I know, Penny, I feel that way about our little house too. It's the only real home I've ever had. But wherever Brad is, that's where my home should be. Doesn't even the Bible say that or something like it? 'Where your heart is, there also will be your treasure?' Brad is my heart — and Belinda. If he wants to go. . . ." Her voice trailed away tremulously; her beautiful eyes glistened with tears. "If that happens, Penny —" Thea bit her lower lip, then added earnestly, "— it would make all the difference in the world to me, Penny, if you'd say yes. Of course, I know you'd have to think about it, but there'd be plenty of time for that. Brad has to find out all about what he'd have to get to take and all. But if I thought you were going too, well. . . ."

Thea did not finish her sentence. She didn't need to. Penny understood. She and Thea had been inseparable since childhood, more like sisters than friends. Even now that they were grown up, hardly a day passed that they didn't spend at least part of it together.

For a minute they were both silent. The only sound was the ticking of the wall clock, which seemed suddenly loud. After a while, Thea got to her feet and took her empty glass over to the drain board. She paused and placed her hand on Penny's shoulder. "Please, Penny, at least think about it — I mean, about coming to church tonight."

Immediately Penny felt a reluctance to attend, as if by going she would be making some kind of commitment. So she put off giving Thea a definite answer by saying, "I can't promise. I'll have to wait and see if Grams feels up to it when she gets home from the quilting bee."

15

Thea's sigh was resigned, as she knew that was all she was going to get from Penny at the moment. "Well, I better wake Belinda up and be on my way. Brad wants an early supper so we can get to church and get seats near the front. It's bound to be crowded. Posters have been put all over town about Brother Carmichael's talk tonight."

A few minutes later Thea emerged from the downstairs bedroom carrying Belinda. Penny touched her niece's tousled curls, and Belinda removed her thumb from her mouth long enough to give a dimpled smile.

Penny walked with them to the door and out onto the porch.

Thea shifted Belinda to her other hip and went down the steps. At the bottom she turned back to Penny. "You *will* try to come tonight, won't you, Penny? And promise you'll think about what I said, won't you?"

Penny didn't like being pressured. Thea had always depended on her. How many times in their long friendship had Thea persuaded her to do something she didn't want to do, go someplace she hadn't planned to go? Penny didn't want to be placed in that position now. But it was hard to turn down Thea's pleading eyes. And this time there was an anxiety about her request that Penny was quick to hear. She knew her so well. Instinctively she responded to that anxiety and said, "Yes, I'll try."

Still standing there, leaning on the porch railing, Penny watched Thea go out the gate. Just beyond a grove of alders Thea turned, took Belinda's chubby little hand in hers, and waved. Penny waved back. Her heart gave a funny little twist. She loved them both so much. How would it feel if Thea's guess was right? If Brad really intended to go west? Instantly Penny felt the loneliness that would be hers. She took a long breath. "Drat that brother of mine! Why is he never content? Maybe this is just one of his passing phases — like so many others he's had over the years. Maybe."

Back in the house, Penny stirred up the fire in the stove. Grams would be home soon, and if, as she'd half promised Thea, they went to the church meeting tonight, she better get things started for an early supper.

While setting the table Penny thought over her conversation with her sister-in-law. Thea wasn't given to imagining things. If she thought Brad was serious about going out west, he probably *was*. Why hadn't he said anything to Grams or to her? Probably afraid one of them would dash cold water on the idea. California. She had to admit the name

17

brought a tingle of excitement. She too had heard all the rumors, repeated by people who'd gone to the lecture last week. "Oranges big as melons growing on trees! Richest farmland you can imagine. Gold shimmering in creeks so you just have to scoop in your hand and bring out a fistful." The idea of it *did* send a tingle of excitement through her. Her brother wasn't the only one in the family who had an adventurous streak.

As a child Penny could run, jump, climb trees, and ride horseback as well as Brad and some of his friends. She was always quick to issue a challenge or take a dare with the best of them. Grams had finally called a halt to her "hoydenish shenanigans" when Penny was thirteen, declaring it was "time she put down her hems, put up her hair, and start acting like a young lady."

As Penny got out the potatoes, peeled them, and put them on to boil, she thought of some of her wilder exploits — ones Grams had never got wind of. With a smile she was remembering them as the door opened and her grandmother came into the house. Penny gave a guilty start.

"Oh, Grams, it's you!"

Cordelia Sayres gave her granddaughter a curious glance. "Who else would it be?" she asked tartly.

Quickly dropping her paring knife and wiping her hands, Penny hurried over to help her grandmother off with her shawl, taking the basket of quilting patches from her. "Did you have a nice time? How were all the ladies?"

"Needles going as fast as tongues," chuckled Grams, handing Penny her bonnet to hang up. "And what have you been up to?"

"Thea came over and we went berry picking. We got lots for you. I started supper, because Thea wants us to go hear the special speaker at church this evening. Seems Brad's all het up 'bout California." Without saying just *how* interested Brad possibly was, Penny went on, "I told her I wasn't sure. I said you might be too tired to go. Are you?"

Grams pursed her lips thoughtfully. "Hmm, the ladies were talking about that this afternoon. Brother Carmichael's his name. Seems like everybody's plannin' to attend. So I suppose we shouldn't miss it."

"We don't *have* to go, that is, if you're too tired, Grams?"

"You're the one who don't seem too anxious, miss. Don't *you* want to go?"

Feeling disloyal to Thea, Penny quickly assured her, "Oh, I'll go. I just told Thea that I'd make sure *you* felt up to it — no, ma'am, I'll be glad to go."

"Then that's settled," Grams said, tying on

her apron and moving over to the stove.

Penny knew it would have taken only a little more persuasion on her part to convince Grams not to go. But from what Thea had implied about Brad, maybe Grams *should* hear all that this Brother Carmichael had to say. Then she would be in a better position to judge what Brad had in mind. Even though he was a married man and had left home three years ago, Penny knew her brother still had great respect for their grandmother's judgment.

Grams had taken them in and reared them after their mother's death and their widowed father's fatal logging accident just one year later. To six-year-old Penny and her brother, who was then nine, Grams had given them more than a home. She had given them a sense of belonging, a feeling that they were special, the security of discipline, as well as concern and love. Somehow Penny felt it was important for Grams to advise Brad if he really was thinking of pulling up stakes and going west.

After supper Penny cleared the table, then said, "I'll go get ready," and went upstairs to her loft bedroom. Ever since she had first come to live with Grams this room had been her special place. Dormer windows looked out through the boughs of towering pine trees to the lake just beyond the end of the property. Its slanted roof gave her a cozy sense of privacy, her imaginative fancy play, like a princess in a tower.

She changed into a green merino dress, trimmed with darker green braid, and took her bonnet off its stand on the bureau. As she did, her glance fell on the framed daguerreotype of her parents taken on their wedding day. Her mother had been what Grams called an "Irish beauty": dark, wavy hair; rose and cream complexion; and emerald green eyes. From the oval perfection of her mother's face, Penny critically surveyed her own face in the mirror. No resemblance. None at all. *She* had taken after her father's family. She was tall for a girl and boyishly slim; her eyes were slate blue; her nose too long and her mouth too wide. Thankfully her hair had darkened from vivid carrot color to auburn. But she had the kind of fair skin, sprinkled with freckles, that goes with red hair.

It was ironic that throughout her growing up years her best friend was the prettiest girl in Dunwoodie! Althea Rawlings. If Thea hadn't been such a dear, sweet-natured person, Penny might have been jealous. Their friendship bond had been forged early as they both were left motherless.

Thea's father had remarried less than a year

after her mother had died. Her stepmother, Veda, was a stern, unloving woman. The only warmth, affection, and acceptance Thea received was here in Grams' house. Even now, as a grown woman, wife, and mother, Thea was still emotionally dependent. In fact, Penny had always found it hard to refuse Thea anything. Like going to church tonight!

With a sigh, Penny put on her bonnet. Tying the ribbons firmly under her square chin, she made a grimace at her image. Then she forced a saccharine smile that widened as she observed that at least her teeth were white and straight. People said she had a nice smile.

When Penny and Grams arrived they saw the small wooden church was unusually crowded for a midweek service. News of this speaker, recently arrived from the West, had spread quickly throughout the community. Interest in the westward movement was already high, which was probably why more men were present than ordinarily came for the Wednesday night prayer meeting.

As Penny and her grandmother approached the church, a tall, young man detached himself from the group of men talking in the churchyard and came diffidently forward.

"Evenin', Mrs. Sayres." Todd Farnum

touched the brim of his hat, then added shyly, "Evenin', Penny."

"Well, Todd, what a surprise to see *you* here on a Wednesday night." Penny's eyes twinkled mischievously. "You suddenly got religion or California fever?"

Grams gave her a sharp nudge with her elbow. "Penny! What a thing to say!"

Undaunted, Penny kept looking at Todd as if for an explanation. *"Well?"*

Obviously discomfited by Penny's words, Todd shifted from one foot to the other, stammering, "Can't rightly say. . . ."

Penny laughed, but her grandmother told him, "Don't pay a bit of mind to her, Todd. She's got a wicked tongue for teasin'. Whatever your reason for comin', it's nice to see you. How's your ma?"

"Doin' much better, ma'am, thank you kindly."

Penny's eyes still sparkled with merriment. Todd should be used to her having fun at his expense. They had been playmates as children, going all through school together. In age he was between her and Brad. Now that they'd grown up, Todd would have preferred their friendship to become a courtship. Even Penny was aware that most of Dunwoodie expected them to marry someday. But not *her.* Marriage was a long way off in Penny's future.

To Gram's annoyed and vocal despair, Penny — even at twenty, an age when many a Dunwoodie girl started worrying that she was moving perilously close to being an "old maid" — was in no hurry. Several young men had tried courting her, but none more persistently than Todd Farnum. So far none had been successful. Grams said it was because she was too independent and outspoken: "You'll never get a man to put up with that, young lady," she would caution. But Penny would retort, "Flirting is silly and being coy worse. If a man doesn't like me the way I am, I wouldn't be interested in spending the rest of my life with him anyway!"

To Penny, the idea of settling down to domesticity did not have the appeal it had to most of the girls she knew. There always seemed to be something beckoning from some distant horizon, just over the hill, like music only faintly heard. Oh, she knew she was a daydreamer; she'd been told that often enough. Maybe it was the Irish blood in her veins, inherited from her mother, that made her like that: Ireland, the faraway land of poets and saints. Well, not the saint part, but perhaps she had a bit of poetry in her soul — or as Grams might say acerbically, "A bit of blarney."

After a few more pleasantries they left Todd

and went up the steps into the vestibule. As she entered the church, Penny saw Jeremiah Bradshaw out of the corner of her eye, and she felt a pang of dismay. She had to suppress a shudder. She hoped he hadn't seen them come in, for he would surely try to join them in the same pew. Taking a firm hold of Grams' arm, Penny steered her to the opposite side of the church, and as she did, she received an irritated glance from the independent little lady. Once they were seated, Grams remonstrated in a whisper, "For pity's sake, Penny, why did you push me like that — as though I can't manage on my own!"

Penny didn't want to explain, so she just whispered, "Sorry." Still, she had the feeling that Jeremiah *had* seen them, and she felt a tingling sensation along the back of her neck, an awareness that she was being observed. Why did she have such an aversion to him?

There was just something about him. Was it his fawning overeagerness, his almost uncanny ability to spot her at any gathering, to appear at her side instantly on countless occasions, making no effort to conceal his attraction? It was an attraction she certainly did not return. Was it this unwanted attention that made her so uncomfortable? Or was it something more? Something that made her skin crawl, made her want to draw away from any

25

contact with him? Worse still, nothing seemed to discourage him. No matter how cool she was, he persisted in pursuing her.

To make matters worse, everyone else seemed to think Jeremiah Bradshaw a fine, upstanding young man and considered him an eligible bachelor. In the eyes of most of the town's matchmakers, he was a "good catch." He was well educated, by Dunwoodie standards, having gone off to college for two years, and was now a clerk in the County Recording Office. He was well mannered and good-looking. Tall with even features and dark, wavy hair and gray eyes with long lashes any girl might envy. No one, not even Grams, could understand why Penny would not be flattered by his interest.

But when he looked at her, Penny felt like shivering. How could she say what only she sensed? Something frightening behind the ingratiating manner, a cold shrewdness in those eyes? The feeling that he was manipulative and could not be trusted?

Even as she thought about this, Penny felt irresistibly drawn to glance his way. To her horror Jeremiah was staring at her. The minute their eyes met, Penny immediately averted her head, but not before he had smiled. A smile that sent an icy sliver of repulsion all through her. Why didn't he find some other girl who might welcome his attentions?

Gradually the hum of voices dimmed to a murmur. The rustle of people finding seats and settling into place began to quiet. A hush of anticipation fell as Reverend Thomas came into the pulpit to introduce the speaker.

"Brothers and sisters, tonight we are going to hear an amazing story, told by a person who has seen some of the glories of God's creation that none of us here have seen. He's come back with a vision to share with us. I feel sure you'll be astonished and inspired by what he is going to tell us tonight." He turned to the tall, lean man who had accompanied him to the front of the church. "Brother Willis Carmichael, will you come forth now?"

The craggy-faced man stood behind the lectern and began to speak in a dramatic voice. He talked of the splendor of mountains, the vast plains, the rivers brimming with an abundance of fish, the forests thick with game and wildlife of all kinds, rich land to be farmed. . . . Penny listened but only half believed what the man was saying. Was it truly possible that the place he was describing could be the modern version of the biblical "Promised Land," as he declared? It sounded almost too good to be true. Yet she could feel all around her the readiness to accept the picture he was painting — especially in the men. They were leaning in their seats toward Brother Carmichael, hanging on his every word.

The enthusiasm *was* contagious, however. Penny could feel the excitement stirring among the congregation. Brother Carmichael appealed to every man and woman in his audience who had ever felt the frustration, the drabness, the workaday ordinariness of their lives. He was offering them a chance to change their lives in a glorious way.

Then, Brother Carmichael leaned forward on the pulpit and his voice deepened dramatically. "But, my friends, in all this manifestation of God's creation, his providence, his bounty, there lies a profound need. A need that cries out to be filled. There are some of you here tonight who will hear and respond to that call. I beseech you to search your hearts and souls and discover if the Lord God is asking you to forsake all and go out west to minister to these poor souls. . . ." Brother Carmichael's voice broke as he struggled to continue. "Oh, my brethren," he intoned, "if ever there were fields white for the harvest, it is in the western territories, where Indians live under savage conditions, long deprived of the refreshing waters of baptism, the breath of the Spirit. The opportunities are enormous for those willing to sacrifice their comfortable lives in this part of our beloved country to track new pathways of salvation for those less fortunate ones who have never heard the reviving words of the gospel. For you few who respond generously, there are blessings awaiting you here on earth in a glorious new, unspoiled land out west, just as later on there will also be eternal rewards."

Having concluded, Brother Carmichael came down from the podium. Immediately he was surrounded by people anxious to ask questions and find out more information.

Grams had nodded off during some of the more repetitive parts of the talk, so when Penny whispered, "Let's go," she was ready to leave. Penny saw Brad among those clustered around the speaker. Thea was sitting in one of the front pews, holding a sleeping Belinda in her lap, patiently waiting. There was no real opportunity to talk to either of them. Knowing Thea would surely tell her their reactions later, Penny maneuvered Grams toward the back of the church and out the door, hoping also to escape Jeremiah.

Outside, on the church steps, however, Jeremiah was waiting. He courteously greeted her grandmother first. "Good evening, Mrs. Sayres. Good evening, Penny." Instinctively Penny stiffened, suppressing an involuntary shudder. He went on smoothly: "May I have the pleasure of escorting you home?"

Penny started to give Grams' arm a warning pinch, but it was too late. Jeremiah had already offered his arm to Grams, who had taken it. There was nothing Penny could do. Luckily it was only a short walk. As the three of them walked back along the moonlit streets, Jeremiah began expounding. "What a powerful message, wouldn't you say? I was most impressed, weren't you?" Not pausing for her answer, he continued, "I certainly need time to ponder some of the things he spoke of, weigh them carefully. He has certainly given *all* of us something to think about."

Penny checked the urge to make some sarcastic remark. Jeremiah was *so* pretentious it set her teeth on edge. Was she the only one who saw through Jeremiah? Always trying to impress, as though he had deeper insight than anyone else? It was not too soon for Penny when they reached their front gate.

"Thank you for seeing us home, Mr. Bradshaw," Grams said politely. "Since it's rather late, I won't ask you in this evening."

"Of course, Mrs. Sayres, I understand," Jeremiah replied, then added insinuatingly, "But *another* time, perhaps?"

"Of course. We'd be most pleased." Grams

nodded, and Jeremiah unlatched the gate for them both to pass through.

"I'll look forward to it with great pleasure," his voice followed them.

The minute they were inside and the front door closed, Penny gave an exasperated moan and demanded, "Oh, Grams, why ever did you invite him for? You know I cannot abide the man!"

Grams looked shocked. "Well, now, miss. It's still *my* house, I reckon, and I can invite whoever I like, I should think. What did you expect me to say when he practically invited himself?" Grams untied her bonnet strings and patted her gray coronet of braids, then hung up her shawl and started for the kitchen. Over her shoulder she said, "Your hoity-toity ways are not going to keep me from employing common courtesy, miss! And why do you have such an aversion to him? Mr. Bradshaw seems nice enough to me and if you weren't so persnickety you'd acknowledge that. Why, some girls would be mighty flattered that such a gentlemanly fellow was paying them some attention."

"Well, I'm *not*. So be sure to let me know when you issue him an invitation so that *I* can be *sure* not to be here!"

Grams threw Penny a disapproving glance but didn't say anything. She put the kettle on and got out an apple pie from the pie safe and proceeded to cut two slices.

Grams' silence always spoke volumes. Penny knew she had been rude. Contrite, she went behind her grandmother, put her arms around her plump waist and gave her a hug.

"I'm sorry, Grams. But, I can't help it. There's just something about Jeremiah Bradshaw —"

"Well, then, why were you so unkind to poor Todd Farnum?"

"*Unkind?* I wasn't unkind! Todd knows when I'm teasing. Why, I've known him forever —"

"He's not still a boy that you can tease and torment, miss. He's a grown man, and he's got a fine farm and a good head on his shoulders. And if you don't watch that tongue of yours, you'll be left on the shelf."

"Left on the shelf? What on earth does *that* mean?" Penny grinned, knowing very well what it meant. With an impudent flounce of her tiered skirt she sat down on one of the chairs at the round kitchen table and stared at her grandmother with widened eyes.

Grams sniffed. "It *means,* miss, for your information, all the eligible men in this town will be gone to girls smarter than you — at least smart enough to keep their mouths shut and not spout out the first silly thing that comes into their heads to say. *That's* what it means, Miss Know-It-All!" She emphasized her statement by setting the plate of pie down in front of Penny with a little click.

"Maybe I don't want to get married, Grams." Penny shrugged. "Maybe I'd be perfectly happy to be a spinster."

Grams poured the water from the hissing kettle into the teapot, which had been kept warm at the back of the stove. Then she took a seat opposite Penny, regarding her over her spectacles for a long moment before replying, "I've heard ducks quack before."

Penny knew better than to continue this line of discussion. Instead she took a bite of her pie and asked, "So, what did you think of Brother Carmichael and his talk?"

Her grandmother stirred sugar into her teacup thoughtfully. "I feel he's going to stir up a great deal of unrest in the community. Firing up men with dreams of free land, all that sunshine and fruit growing so easy, to say nothing of gold just lying there waiting to be scooped up. . . . Didn't say much about how long that journey is, what hardships there would be for women and children along the way. . . . I don't know, Penny, but I'm a little wary of people who talk about pots of gold at the end of the rainbow and fancy it up with spiritual calling. . . ."

"You saw Brad up there with the first of them, didn't you?"

"Yes, I did, and Brad's just the kind that would be taken in by it all."

"He's *already* interested, Grams. Even before tonight. Thea told me he's been talking a lot about it. He's read all the accounts in the paper. Says he's become more and more discontent with what he calls his 'dead-end life' here in Dunwoodie. Keeps saying out west things would be different. Thea says he's rarin' to go. . . ." Penny paused with a forkful of pie halfway to her mouth. "But I don't think *she's* all that eager to go."

"And why *should* she be? She's got a nice house, a sweet little baby, family and friends nearby. Why would she want to pack up and go God knows where?"

"But if Brad wants to go —"

"If that's what her husband wants to do, Thea will go, I expect," Grams sighed. "She'll do what all women through the ages have done: follow her man."

Penny didn't comment. Her grandmother's declaration conveyed exactly why *she* wasn't in any hurry to marry and give up her independence.

Chapter 2

Penny woke up the next morning feeling out of sorts. The meeting the night before had been unsettling. She felt disturbed by Brother Carmichael's oratory and particularly the men's reaction to his talk — especially Brad's. She had the same worries Grams had about her brother. Brad was easily influenced and likely to be carried away by the extravagant claims made for the distant land of California. Coupled with Thea's suspicions, the eloquent descriptions of the night before might have been the proverbial last straw. Much as Penny loved her brother, over the years she had observed that his impulsiveness was often followed by a quick loss of interest. Still, she was wary that his restlessness might cause him to do something foolhardy. Penny recalled how Brad's eyes were shining with excitement last night. And Thea — well, she had looked anxious and unhappy.

Penny punched the pillows behind her head and frowned. Thea wasn't cut out for months of roughing it on a long wagon train journey. Penny knew Thea better than anyone. From the time they were both six years old and Penny had spotted the shy little girl standing on the edge of the schoolyard on the first day of school, she had kept a protective eye on Thea. Even after Thea had married Brad, Penny remained her confidante and closest friend. It was more than anxiety Penny had seen in Thea's eyes. That's what worried Penny most. Something else was troubling Thea, and Penny didn't know what.

Penny heard movement in the kitchen downstairs; the smell of coffee and bacon frying wafted up the stairwell. In spite of going to bed later than usual, Grams had probably been up since dawn. Penny knew she should be down there too, bringing in more wood for the stove and getting water from the well, although it sounded as if Grams had already done so. Although she seemed as spry and active as ever, Grams wasn't getting any younger.

"Penny!" Grams' voice called from the bottom of the steps. "Are you going to be a slugabed this morning? Breakfast's almost ready. I'm taking the biscuits out now."

"Coming, Grams!" Guiltily Penny threw the covers back and got up. As she washed and dressed, Penny kept thinking of the real possibility that Brad was planning to join the

36

trek west. Brad was so enthusiastic, and optimistic to a fault. What really bothered Penny was that she knew he could talk Thea into going against her wishes and even against her better judgment. His own excitement was infectious. Grams said he could talk bugs off a potato vine.

Maybe she should stop fretting over Brad and Thea's plans. No matter what *she* thought, Brad would make the decision and Thea would go along with it. But why did Penny have the distinct impression Thea was terrified of the whole idea? Was there some secret reason she hadn't said?

Penny poured water from the pitcher into her washbowl, splashed her face several times. As she dried it she looked at herself in the round mirror above the pine washstand. Instead of her own, it seemed as though she saw Thea's delicate face, the violet blue eyes staring back pleadingly. What was she trying to say?

"Penny, food's getting cold. You comin'?" Grams' voice came again.

"Coming!" Penny tossed the face towel aside and ran down the steps. She had just seated herself at the table and begun eating her scrambled eggs when she heard footsteps on the porch. A minute later the front door opened and Brad walked in. If Penny felt *she* had been short-changed on looks, her brother had not. Brad Sayres was tall, well built. He had a wide, friendly smile and intensely blue eyes that shone with good humor from his handsome, sun-tanned face.

"Mornin', Grams! Sis!" he greeted them cheerfully.

He sauntered over to the stove as casually as if he still lived here. He lifted the lid on one of the pots and inhaled rapturously. "Ummm, smells mighty fine, Grams. Marmalade?"

"Yes, it is. Help yourself to some coffee, boy. Or would you want some bacon and eggs?"

"No thanks, Grams. Had breakfast. However, ..." He straddled the bench on the other side of the table and reached into the basket, covered with a blue checked cloth. "I think I'll just have one of these biscuits . . . if I may?"

"What brings you out and over here so early?" Penny asked, a funny premonition stirring in her mind.

Brad took his time, slathering butter onto his biscuit and taking a bite before answering. "Well, now . . . I was kinda curious how you all reacted to Brother Carmichael last night. Didn't see you afterwards . . . left pretty quick, didn't you? Why? Not interested? Didn't like him?"

Grams exchanged a glance with Penny, then said, "Oh, he seemed sincere enough, I'm sure. But my goodness, Brad, could California be all that wonderful? He made it sound like the Garden of Eden before the fall."

"Well, he ought to know, Grams. He's been out there twice. Made the trip two times."

"If it's all that great, why don't he stay?"

"Yes, why not?" Penny joined in.

Brad's eyes, so much like Penny's, twinkled as his voice took on an oratorical tone. "He came to bring the message. Didn't you hear him say? 'Fields white for the harvest' and all that?"

"Don't tell me *you're* thinking about becoming a missionary?" Penny blinked with exaggerated disbelief.

Ignoring his sister's sarcasm, Brad grinned, "I believe I'd like a cup of coffee, Grams."

"I'll get it," Penny said and rose, giving her brother a dubious look.

"He *was* pretty eloquent, I must say," Grams commented dryly.

"Well, Grams, maybe you didn't know, but I was pretty interested in the West *before* Brother Carmichael came," Brad said as he accepted the steaming mug Penny handed him. "But I thought if Thea heard it preached about in church, she might be more willing to think about *us* going."

Grams set down her own fork and stared at her grandson. "You mean you're *really* thinking about it?"

"I'm doing more than thinking about it, Grams. I'm going. I'm putting the house up for sale. I'm goin' to start buildin' a wagon and be ready to join a wagon train leaving from Independence in the spring."

"And what does Thea say about all this?" gasped Penny.

"She's all for it," Brad answered blithely, then amended, "at least, she's all for it if that's what I want to do. But I want to do what's best for *us*. It's the greatest opportunity young people ever had since the first settlers came here. But here in Dunwoodie, opportunities are limited. You know that, Grams. I'd never get enough money together to buy a farm of any size — or land. In California you can get government land for a low down payment on a homestead. Acres and acres of prime farm land for the taking . . . you just have to live on it for a full year and —"

"But it's such a long way. It's so far and. . . ." Grams' voice wavered a little.

"You could come with us, Grams."

"Not me, son, I'm too old, too set in my ways. I've lived in this house since I was sev-

40

enteen when I came here as a bride, I had all my children here, including your father. I raised 'em here, lost 'em here. I plan to end my days here. . . . Besides, I couldn't leave your Uncle Billy."

Uncle Billy was Gram's younger brother who had been disabled by a hunting accident years before. He lived in a small cabin by himself nearby, and although fiercely independent, he took supper with them several times a week and was a part of the close-knit clan.

Brad glanced over at Penny. "What about *you*, sis? Doesn't the idea tickle *your* adventurous streak? Thea would be even more willing to go if you'd come along."

Penny didn't want to betray the fact Thea had already broached that subject. She needed more time to think about it. She still felt she didn't know the whole story; Thea was holding something back.

"*Me?*" she echoed as if she'd never heard the suggestion.

"Sure, why not? Might even find you a husband," he teased.

"Who says I want one?" she retorted.

"Well, old Todd's still moonin' away for you, come to that. I know Todd's seriously thinking about going too. We could make us up a party, two wagons —"

"Oh, hush! How many times do I have to

41

tell everyone? Todd's a friend, not a beau!"

"Not to hear him tell it!" Brad retorted. "Then what about Jeremiah Bradshaw? Nobody could miss those calves' eyes he's castin' your way every time you're in sight."

Irritated, Penny balled up her napkin and aimed it at him. He ducked, laughing, caught it and threw it back.

"Now, stop it, you two. Looky here. You're not young'uns anymore," Grams said with mock severity. But her eyes were merry behind her glasses, and her mouth tugged at the corners trying not to smile.

Brad glanced over at Penny. "I'm serious, sis. It would be great if you decided to come along."

"Could I bring Mariah?" she parried. Mariah was her saddle horse, given for her fourteenth birthday, a gentle dappled-gray mare.

"Sure thing," Brad nodded. "Think it over? A once-in-a-lifetime adventure?" he grinned. "Better'n just readin' all those romance novels."

That was all that was said about it then. Brad launched into some further details of what he had learned about the necessary preparations for the overland journey west. Grams and Penny listened without making further comments.

After Brad left, Grams poured them each a second cup of coffee, something she didn't usually do. Usually she was up and busy getting to her next chore. Bringing their cups back to the table, she sat down, folded her arms, and leaned forward on them. She asked Penny, "Well, what do you think, honey? Want to go along on the great adventure? Or are you waiting to see if Todd Farnum's going to join the Westward-Ho bunch?"

"Todd? Oh, Grams, that's just Brad's foolishness."

"Not altogether, missy, so don't play the innocent with me." She fastened her eyes on her granddaughter so that Penny couldn't look away. "What Brad said is just what everyone in Dunwoodie knows. Todd's been sweet on you since you were out of pinafores and pantaloons. Are you waiting to see if he's going to propose marriage or a wagon train trip to California?"

"I don't think Todd has any notion of going west." Penny shook her head. "And he certainly hasn't asked me to marry him. And even if he did — either one of those things — well, his decision wouldn't have anything to do with *mine*."

Grams raised her eyebrows. "Oh, I've no doubt of that. You're not like Thea, who jumps when Brad snaps his fingers."

"You think that's wrong?"

"Not wrong. No, not at all. Not for Thea. But you're a different story. You've always had a mind of your own since you were knee-high to a grasshopper. And although Todd's a fine fellow, I'm not sure he's the right one for you."

"Why not?"

"Maybe because he'd be too easy for you to lead around, for one. But mostly because I think, in your own way, you're as adventurous as Brad. I think you've a hankering for new sights, new places, new challenges. And until that's out of your system, I can't see you settlin' down with someone as placid as Todd." Grams finished her coffee, then got to her feet, and with a crumpled cloth napkin wiped up the damp ring it had made on the table. "Remember, you marry the life as well as the man. If you have any doubts about marrying anyone, it's better by far to wait. To do otherwise would bring misery on both of you."

"Why, Grams, just last night you were warning me about being 'left on the shelf.' "

"Well, maybe I changed my mind. I'm an open person, always ready to listen, to see things from another view . . . and that's what I've done." Then her tone turned sharp: "Come on, miss, we've got baking to do."

Chapter 3

Brother Carmichael was scheduled to give two more talks in Dunwoodie, one the following night at the Town Hall and another on Sunday at the church. Neither Penny nor Grams planned to attend, and Brad certainly did not need any more encouragement to take off for the West. Penny had heard all she wanted to about California. She had more than a few misgivings about the rich rewards awaiting across the prairies and mountains to the golden West. She was particularly troubled by Thea's silence about the venture on which Brad seemed set to embark. Besides Uncle Billy always took Sunday night supper with them, and the three of them looked forward to their usual good time together. Uncle Billy was a wonderful storyteller, and he and Grams swapped stories about their childhood, each trying to outdo the other.

It was a warm, wonderful evening of family fun. Grams didn't mention Brad's plans to Uncle Billy, and Penny's worries were temporarily put aside. But the next day she was unexpectedly forced to face the whole subject of California.

On Monday afternoon Grams sent Penny to take a basket containing jellies and two loaves of fresh baked bread to a sick friend's house. Mrs. Bristow, confined to her bed for an entire week, was eager to talk and hear all the latest news, so Penny had to stay for a cup of tea and a chat. By the time she started home it was beginning to get dark. Deciding to take a shortcut through the woods, she hurried along the path thick with pine needles. Suddenly she heard a voice call her name: "Penny! Wait, Penny!"

Surprised, she halted and turned to see who it was. A man was running along the trail behind her. *Oh, no!* She felt instant dread. It was Jeremiah Bradshaw! Not waiting for him to catch up, she started walking again briskly.

"Hold on, Penny," he called again.

"I'm in a hurry, Jeremiah," she said over her shoulder.

"But this is really important. I have something important to tell you." He reached her side out of breath. "Actually, it's *providential* that I saw you."

Penny quickened her pace. "I really don't have time to stop and chat, Jeremiah," she said, annoyed. "It's getting late, and Grams will be wondering where I am."

"Wait until you hear what I have to say, Penny," he said, matching his stride to hers. "It's something Brother Carmichael said about —"

"I've heard all I want to hear about California."

"Not *this* you haven't," Jeremiah said, not seeming at all disturbed by the irritated look she gave him. "I'm sorry you and your grandmother weren't there to hear for yourselves." There was a hint of reproach in his voice. "You missed a powerful message —"

"And I've heard all I care to hear of Brother Carmichael's messages as well!" she declared and added, "I have a strong feeling he exaggerates."

"You're wrong, Penny," Jeremiah pronounced solemnly. "Furthermore, there was a *personal* message last night *you* should have heard."

"What do you mean?"

Jeremiah took a few long strides ahead, then turned so that he was facing her so that she had to stop walking. "Listen, Penny. At the close of the meeting Sunday night Brother Carmichael asked each of us to search our hearts to see if God was trying to tell us something. He asked for silence so that we could all quietly examine our minds and souls . . . and —" Jeremiah paused dramatically "— I *did* and . . . Penny," here Jeremiah's voice deepened, "what I got very clearly was that *you* and I should go *together* out west . . . be missionaries."

Stunned, Penny looked at him aghast. "*What?* That's the most ridiculous thing I ever heard! Jeremiah, you must be mistaken."

Satisfied that he had caught her attention, Jeremiah's expression was smug. Penny protested, "I mean, you certainly *are* mistaken. I have no intention of going to California in the first place, much less as a *missionary!*"

Jeremiah shook his head, and his eyes speared into hers. "You can't fight the will of God, Penny. We are to start preparing to go out west and minister to the savages —"

"Jeremiah, I'm not even going to discuss this," Penny said indignantly. She started to walk away from him, but he reached out, caught her by the arm, and swung her around to face him. His eyes were burning, his pupils dilated. Penny's heart began thrumming as Jeremiah's fingers tightened on her arm.

"The Lord has shown me you *are* to be my wife. . . . If you refuse to listen, Penny, you'll pay the price."

Jeremiah was frightening. Penny felt an icy trickle of fear run down her spine. Determined not to show it, she lifted her chin defiantly, "That's impossible! Why would he show *you* this and not *me?*"

"Because you've closed your mind and your heart. You're running away from what you know deep down is his will —"

"I know nothing of the kind, Jeremiah," she said firmly, trying to pull away from him. But he held her fast. His fingers pressed so hard into her arm, even through her wool jacket, that it hurt. "Let me go!"

"You're afraid to admit that you know I'm right, aren't you?" His eyes glinted triumphantly; his mouth twisted in a grotesque smile. He gave a short, ugly laugh. "You're proud, Penny, and that's one of the deadly sins, the one the Devil uses to get people to disobey God. You'll have to come to repentance."

"You're mad, Jeremiah. You don't know what you're talking about. . . ." Combined fear and anger gave her strength, and she yanked hard at the arm he was holding. "Let me go, Jeremiah!"

"Go then!" He let go so suddenly that she was thrown off balance and stumbled backward. "But you won't forget what I told you. I can see that you know it's true, and you will eventually have to bend to God's will for us."

Realizing she was free, she turned and began to run. Jeremiah's voice followed her: "You can't run away from your predestined

49

duty. You'll reap what you sow, Penny. Retribution —," Jeremiah's dire threats echoed hollowly in the woods.

She ran blindly, empty basket bumping against her until the pain in her side made her stop to lean on a tree, gasping for breath. Fearfully she glanced behind her to see if Jeremiah was pursuing her. The woods were darkening fast. Her heart was hammering against her ribs, and the pain was like a dagger, but she was afraid to remain longer. Jeremiah was crazy. She was convinced he had lost his reason.

Then she heard a branch crack, a twig snapping as if a foot had stepped on it. Panicking, Penny picked up her skirts and began running again. In sight of the house, she stopped. Panting, she leaned against the fence post, taking huge gulps of air into her hurting lungs. Her legs were shaking and her breath was coming in short gasps. The fact that she had escaped from the frenzied Jeremiah brought tears of relief. Spontaneous prayers of gratitude sprang up, inarticulate but heartfelt, scattered words from various psalms — "The Lord is my shield, my shelter, a high tower, thank you, Lord."

She felt ravaged by Jeremiah's venom, his scathing words. What right had he to say the things he had? Deep, shuddering tremors shook Penny. But what if — ? She gave her head a little toss, straightened herself. No, she wouldn't even allow herself to think that way. Jeremiah was deranged. He must be if he thought. . . . Penny retied her bonnet strings, adjusted her cape, and went through the gate into the house.

Grams was in the kitchen when she came in the front door. "How was Mrs. Bristow, Penny?" she called.

Penny took a long breath, trying to regain some semblance of calm. She closed her eyes for a few minutes, debating whether or not to tell her grandmother about the experience. Quickly she decided not to upset her and managed to answer, "She's much better, Grams."

Not wanting her grandmother to notice the state she was in, nor ask more questions, Penny went to the stairway and said over her shoulder, "I'll be down in a few minutes." She hurried up the steps. Upon reaching her bedroom she flung herself down on her bed. Penny began to shake. Jeremiah Bradshaw *must* truly be out of his mind! But even if he wasn't, it still had been a terrifying encounter. Gradually her pulses slowed, her breath came more evenly. It was only then she saw that one of the buttons on her jacket sleeve was missing, the dangling thread from it hung reminding her of Jeremiah's viselike grasp, the fierce struggle she had been forced to make to free herself.

With tremendous effort Penny composed herself. She did not want to upset her grandmother. She needed time to think it through, to decide how she could manage to avoid Jeremiah in the future. She certainly did not want a repeat performance of this harrowing confrontation. Of course, he was deluded. Even so, the chilling prediction of what would happen if she didn't accept what he believed made her shudder. She must try to forget about it for now. She'd think of some way to deal with it and *him* later.

After supper, while she and Grams were doing the dishes, Penny asked casually, "Grams, do you believe the Lord gives other people messages intended for you personally?"

Grams went on wiping a plate for a few seconds before answering. "Honey, what I believe is if the Lord wants to tell me something, he does it straight out. He don't need nobody to do it for him. 'Course, you gotta be listening to hear what he has to say. But he don't play guessing games."

Penny breathed a sigh of relief. Coming from Grams, the best Christian she knew, that was reassuring. Most certainly Jeremiah

Bradshaw was crazy. And vindictive too. He resented the fact that she had always discouraged his overtures, refused to allow him to become a 'serious suitor,' even snubbed him overtly when she could. Maybe she hadn't been kind. But how else do you deal with someone who won't take a polite no for an answer? And because he was rejected, he was trying to get to her with this kind of manipulative *religious* ploy.

How terrible to use the Lord for his own purposes. He just wanted to frighten her. She should just forget it, Penny told herself firmly, and put the whole horrible episode out of her mind.

Chapter 4

It was harder than Penny imagined to put the unnerving encounter with Jeremiah out of her mind. She woke up the next morning with a vaguely oppressive feeling. She tried to tell herself that his predictions of disaster were meaningless threats. Or was it remotely *possible* — Penny shuddered — that she really *was* thwarting God's will? No! Penny refused to believe that. Jeremiah was just trying to intimidate her. If he thought he could convince her of something so out of character for her as *that,* he was *very wrong!* Still, Penny could not entirely shake the feeling that something dark was hovering over her. Every once in a while, when she least anticipated it, the memory of that incident in the woods would come back to haunt her.

However, to her great relief she heard something that put the whole disturbing episode into better perspective. She heard Jeremiah had quit his job, left Dunwoodie to join Brother Carmichael on his travels, preaching and lecturing about California. At least she didn't have to be afraid of running into him, feel his reproachful glance upon her, or listen to anymore of his wild "visions." Maybe he would find someone else to fulfill his own dream of going west to "save the heathen Indians."

Besides, Penny had other things to think about. The holidays were coming, a season when there was much baking to be done in preparation for the annual family gathering always held at Grams'. Grams set great store in celebrating both Thanksgiving and Christmas. She did everything to make it special. They decorated the house with pine boughs and holly, got out the best tablecloth and napkins and Grams' best Blue Willow china. Aunts, uncles, cousins, and folks they just called "cousin" and "auntie" even if they were no real kin were invited, and most of them came. Hospitality was for Grams a virtue and a joy. Food was plentiful, talk was constant, music and singing filled the old farmhouse with melody. Uncle Billy played his fiddle for the young folks to dance.

There was also a load more dish washing and cleaning up to be done with all the meals cooked and served. It often turned out that it was Penny and Thea who ended up doing these chores together. They didn't mind, because it gave them a chance to talk.

One evening when they were doing the

dishes, Penny commented, "I sure hear Brad holding forth on the wonders of going west. Talking about 'going to see the elephant,' isn't he? Is it just talk or is he truly serious?"

"Going to see the elephant" was the slang expression everyone used when talking about the great migration to the West. It meant that those who went on the journey would see sights they'd never dreamed of seeing before.

"Oh, he's serious, all right," Thea answered, and she wasn't smiling at Penny's teasing remark. "He's been making lists, drawing up plans to build one of those covered wagons they travel in, figuring out how much equipment and all would cost, how much he could get for our house and —"

Penny halted, drew her hands out of the soapy water, dried them on her apron, placed them on her hips, and stared at Thea. "*Really?* He's *that* serious?"

Thea nodded. "Of course, it wouldn't be until spring that we'd go. That is, if he could sell the house and get everything ready —"

"And how do *you* feel about it?" Penny demanded.

"Well, of course, it's kinda scary to think about — going so far and all. But Brad says it would be wonderful — he's read all about it, and he says our life there would be so much better. There are so many more opportunities for an ambitious man like Brad —"

"Restless, I'd call it," Penny said dryly. "Of course, he talked to Grams and me about it. But that was right after Brother Carmichael was here and — I don't know, I guess I figured it was one of those things he'd got real excited about then forgot. . . ." She let her voice trail off. Evidently her brother hadn't forgotten about it. She looked at her sister-in-law, and suddenly Thea's eyes turned moist with tears.

"Oh, Penny, I hate the thought of leaving you! What will I do without *you?*"

In two seconds the girls were hugging each other. "Why don't you come with us?" Thea asked in a choked voice.

Penny stepped back. "Oh, I couldn't, Thea. Leave Grams?" She shook her head emphatically. "No, I couldn't do that."

Just then one of the uncles came in on his way to the spring house to get another jug of apple cider and stopped to tease and chat with them, so Penny and Thea did not have another chance that evening to pursue the subject.

It was weeks before the two friends had another chance for a private talk. In January Brad's plan to take the big step of traveling by wagon train to California was common knowledge. He wasn't the only Dunwoodie man who had "caught California fever," but he was the only one so far in the small community who was forging ahead with actual preparations to go. He had put their house up for sale and was buying lumber to start building the wagon to specifications for the long journey.

The thought of Thea, her best friend from childhood, as well as her brother and her darling little niece going so far saddened Penny. She tried not to show it around Grams, knowing it was probably equally hard for her. Maybe even more so. At Grams age, saying good-bye to Belinda meant knowing she might never see her again.

Penny's unnatural quietness around the house did not go unnoticed. One cold January morning at breakfast Grams gave Penny a speculative glance. "What on earth ails you lately, girl? You act like you're comin' down with something. Maybe you need a good dose of sulfur and molasses."

"Oh, no, Grams!" Penny put on a horror-stricken face and held up both hands. "The last time you managed to give me that was when I was twelve years old!"

"And I had to chase you halfway round the barn to do it, as I remember!" chuckled her grandmother. "Well, if it ain't that, what's come over you? You sure seem like some-thing's bothering you."

"I guess it's the thought of Brad, Thea, and Belinda leaving come spring."

"Yes, I know, child, but that's life. Least-ways, it is nowadays. Used to be, people stayed put. But not now! Got to go 'see the el-ephant,' I reckon."

Then, late in February, early one afternoon Thea came by, and Grams immediately took possession of Belinda. She took her into her bedroom, where she kept a small box of toys and playthings especially for when Belinda came to the house.

As soon as the two friends were left alone in the kitchen, Thea pulled Penny close. She grabbed her arm and, squeezing it, whis-pered. "Penny, I've got to talk to you. I have something to tell you, but you've got to prom-ise you won't tell a soul."

Penny stared at Thea. "Secrets?"

"Well, yes, at least for a while. But first I have something else to say. Brad and I have talked it over, and we both want you to come with us."

"To California? But I've already told you, Thea, I wouldn't think of leaving Grams."

"Don't say no until you hear all I've got to say, please, Penny. Just think what an adven-ture it would be, and besides, you'd be company for me and a great help with Belinda — Brad agrees with me. He really wants you to come, too. And Grams wouldn't be alone. She never is. Somebody's always visiting here. And there's Uncle Billy. I'm the one who'll be alone if you don't come. And Penny, I really need you —"

Thea's fingers were pressing into Penny's arm. She drew it away, rubbing it as she looked curiously at her sister-in-law. There was something more to all this, but she couldn't figure out just what.

"Is there something you're not telling me, Thea?"

Thea glanced over her shoulder as if afraid she might be overheard, then she drew Penny over to the kitchen table, and they both sat down. In a low, breathless voice Thea began. "First, you've got to promise not to say anything about what I'm going to tell you. Not to *anyone.* Not to Gram, and especially not to Brad."

Penny looked doubtful. "Oh, I don't know —"

"Please, Penny, *please!*" Thea begged. "We've always kept each other's secrets, and this is maybe the most important one I've ever had."

Penny wondered, *Why on earth does Thea seem so frantic? What could be so important?*

Then, seeing the desperation in Thea's eyes, she agreed, "Oh, well, all right. Go ahead."

Thea lowered her voice to a whisper. "Penny, I'm going to have another baby."

Relieved that it wasn't some dark, awful indiscretion she had promised to keep, Penny exclaimed. "Oh, Thea, that's wonderful! A little brother or sister for Belinda. Won't Brad be —," then she broke off and said accusingly, "You haven't told Brad, have you?"

"No. Not yet. And I don't intend to. Not until we're on our way. . . . I'm only a few weeks along, and if he knew. . . ."

"But this changes everything, . . ." began Penny.

"That's just it, it *does*."

"But if he knew about the baby he wouldn't want — oh, Thea, I think you *should* tell Brad," Penny said firmly. "I'm sure it would change his mind . . . at least make him consider waiting until after the baby comes."

"I can't, Penny. Don't you understand? It would spoil everything for him. He's got so many plans. He's pretty sure he's got a buyer for the house, and he's drawing up plans to build our wagon. He's so excited, so optimistic. . . . I just can't do that to him."

Penny would have liked to argue more. But the determination in Thea's face stopped her. As gentle as Thea was, she could be stubborn,

61

and where pleasing Brad was concerned, nothing could move her.

"And how about *you*, Thea? Do you really think this is a good idea? Do you really want to move out west?"

"If it's what Brad wants, I want it too. Brad and Belinda are my whole life, Penny. You of all people ought to know that. Just think what my life was like before Brad loved me."

For a minute both were silent. Images of Thea's stern, unsmiling stepmother came into their minds.

"Besides, going means getting away from Veda." Thea said her stepmother's name with a rare trace of bitterness in her tone. "She's at me all the time, Penny, about Mama's things. She doesn't seem to believe Mama left them to *me* in a separate will. Says they rightfully belong to her because they were in the house when she married Papa."

Penny knew Thea's stepmother to be a stingy, humorless, house-proud woman. She knew how hateful she had been all these years to her friend. It had shown most obviously at the time of her wedding. Everyone was astonished — actually shocked — when the bride showed up at the church wearing *black*. Penny was the only one prepared for *that*. The week before the wedding Thea had come over in tears. Sobbing, she had told Penny that Veda was not willing to spend money for an appropriate bridal gown. "One good black dress is all anyone needs and, what's more, all you're going to get. Foolish expenditure for a fancy outfit you'll only wear once!" Thea quoted her stepmother as saying.

Even so, Thea had been a radiantly beautiful bride — thanks to Penny's grandmother. When she heard about the black wedding dress, she immediately trimmed a scuttle-shaped polished straw bonnet with tiny pink rosebuds and blue forget-me-nots and blue satin ribbons and took it over to Thea the day before the ceremony.

Thea's stepmother had been a grim, unsmiling presence at the wedding. To this day she seemed to try her best to cast a shadow over the young couple's life. The first Mrs. Rawling's possessions, the china, the linens, a rosewood clock, a cedar hope chest, a few pieces of jewelry, still remained a bone of contention between them. Periodically Veda would stir up trouble claiming them.

Thea covered Penny's hands with both her own small ones and pleaded, "I don't mind leaving everything else. In a way, it will be a chance for Brad and me to start a new life together. So you see why I can't let anything stand in Brad's way of having his heart's desire." A tremulous smile lifted the corners of her pretty mouth. " 'Goin' to see the ele-phant.' That's what they call it, you know. The chance of a lifetime to see something you've never seen before. That's why I can't tell him about the baby. You do understand, don't you, Penny?"

Penny was still hesitant. "I don't know. . . ."

"Just until we're on our way, Penny. Then, of course, I'll tell him. He'll be so happy. He wants a son." Thea's smile made her face radiant. "Just think, a son born in *California!*"

Penny had never seen Thea look happier. Maybe that's what life was *really* all about. Loving another person more than yourself, more than what you wanted. A small nagging question in Penny's own heart demanded, *Would I ever love someone that much? Would anyone love me like that?*

"The next part is the *really* important thing, Penny. Please, *please,* think about coming with us." Thea held up her hand as Penny started to protest. "Don't you see, Penny? With a new baby coming — I need you." Thea pressed Penny's hands tightly. "So will you? Think about it seriously?"

"But Thea, there's Grams. What about Grams? For both of us — *all of us* — Brad, me, you, and *Belinda* — you know she adores the baby! To just go off and leave her alone. . . ."

"She could come too! But of course, she

wouldn't leave Uncle Billy, I guess. But he has Aunt Betsy and Aunt Dora too. And so many friends. It wouldn't be like he was completely by himself," Thea countered. "I think she'd want you to go, Penny. And it wouldn't be forever. If you don't like it after we get to California, you can always come back."

"Well, all right, I'll think about it!"

"Oh, wonderful! Thank you, Penny." Thea hugged her, then jumped up. "I better be going. I've a million things to do." She started toward the kitchen door to go out to the garden when she turned back and putting her forefinger to her lips, asked, "And you do promise not to tell?"

Reluctantly Penny nodded.

Chapter 5

Penny's promise to Thea lay heavy on her heart. Whether she should have made it at all worried her. Especially troubling was keeping something so important from Grams. Even more burdensome was Penny's other secret; she still hadn't told her grandmother her decision to go west with Brad and Thea. After much inner struggle, she had decided to go. That Grams was nearing seventy made it harder. In the last two years Penny had taken on the heavier household chores: chopping firewood, bringing water in from the well, filling the copper tubs for the weekly washing, lugging out baskets loaded with wet laundry, hanging it out. Could Grams manage without her? Was Thea's need really greater? She realized in good conscience that she couldn't delay telling her much longer.

The morning she knew she couldn't put it off any longer, Penny puttered around the kitchen, making busy work. Grams sent a couple of curious glances her way but didn't say anything until Penny blurted out her news. Grams was standing at the stove, her back to her, and for a minute after the words were out, Grams seemed to stiffen. Then, a moment later, she turned and, to Penny's astonishment, she didn't seem too surprised. Still holding the pancake turner she nodded briskly and said, "So you've made up your mind at last, have you?"

"How did you . . . ?"

"Well, I figured something was brewing," Grams replied. "You've been mighty quiet lately, and *that's* not like you. I thought you must have something pretty serious on your mind." Then, spearing Penny with her "now tell the truth" look, she asked, "Was this your own idea?"

"Yes," Penny answered. "Of course, both Thea and Brad have asked me to go with them. . . ."

Grams again surprised her by saying, "Well, I think it's a good idea. You're young and strong. You'll be a good support to both of them. Besides there'll be enough work for the two of you keeping tabs on Belinda at her age." Grams seemed about to add something else, then must have thought better of it and just gave a firm nod of her head. "The more I think about it, the better idea it seems to me that you go along. You've got a good head on your shoulders, and Brad needs some balance; he's often apt to go off like a firecracker, and Thea'd rather perish than cross him." Penny knew Grams had hit the proverbial nail on the head. No matter how unhappy Brad's decision might make her, Thea would never refuse to go.

Later, when Penny told Thea she would definitely go with them, Thea was ecstatic. She grabbed and hugged her, and the two of them danced around Thea's kitchen a few times. "Oh, Penny, I think I would have died if you hadn't said yes. I couldn't bear the thought of leaving you behind. You're my best friend. I can't imagine my life without you. And it'll be such an adventure and you and I will have such fun and Belinda will be so happy her Auntie Penny is going too. Oh, Penny, I promise you, you won't regret it."

Thea's use of the word "regret" made Penny think of the ugly scene with Jeremiah. "Regret" was the same word Jeremiah Bradshaw had flung at her for not accepting that *he* had received a word from the Lord that *they* should be married and go to the West as missionaries. In spite of Thea's assurance, Penny had an uneasy feeling that she *might* regret both agreeing to go *and* keeping Thea's secret. As a troubling afterthought, she wondered what Jeremiah Bradshaw would say when he learned she was going west after all.

Penny was relieved she had finally broken the news to Grams. But she still felt uncomfortable hiding the *real* reason she was going. Grams deserved the whole truth. Surely she had the right to know. Grams loved Thea like her own and would welcome the prospect of a new grandbaby.

Even though she was committed to going, at least once a day Penny voiced her concern about leaving her grandmother. She would say, tentatively, "You're sure you won't be too lonely, Grams? Maybe I shouldn't —"

Finally Grams became exasperated. "Don't be silly, child. I'm not in my dotage. Leastways, not yet. And Uncle Billy'll help out much as he can. And Sister Dora and Cousin Tom don't live so far that they can't come over and give me a hand if I need it. Not that I won't miss you. I certainly will . . . but it won't be forever, now, will it?"

"No, Grams, just until they're settled and then. . . ."

That was what Penny and Thea had agreed upon. Yet no real plans of how Penny would come back east were actually discussed.

Penny found herself repeating that same assurance to Todd Farnum one evening when he came by to check for himself on the rumor he'd heard. Penny was out by the stable, grooming her mare, Mariah, when Todd arrived. He stood awkwardly for a few minutes, making circles in the loose dirt with the toe of his boot before he asked, "Is it true? Are you going along with Brad and Thea to California?"

"Yes, I'm going, to help on the journey and to get them settled. With the baby and all. . . ." She went on brushing Mariah's mane. Glancing at Todd, she was shocked at how stunned he looked.

"I don't know about that, Penny."

"About what?"

"That's a mighty long way to travel to turn around and come right back. Are you *sure* this is what you mean to do?"

"Yes, I'm sure, Todd," Penny said gently, then added, "It's not as if it's forever."

Todd shook his head.

"I don't know, Penny. I have a feeling it *is* forever. I don't think you'll come back."

For some reason Penny couldn't try to convince him that she would. The words wouldn't come. Todd looked at Penny with hopeless longing. Although his emotions ran deep, he didn't have the ability to express them. He'd known her so long, loved her ever since . . . well, since he knew what that meant.

They had been children together, climbed trees, ridden horseback, waded in the creek and gone fishing. Everyone in Dunwoodie — except Penny evidently — expected that they would likely marry someday. At this moment, any chance of that happening slipped away, and now that she was out of reach, she seemed even more desirable to Todd than ever.

"Well, I reckon, I'll be going." Todd's disappointment made his voice thick. He took a few steps, then turned back. "I just hope you won't regret it."

Penny watched him walk away. Regret? *Regret!* That word again! She started vigorously wielding the curry brush. She was tired of hearing it. Hadn't she read somewhere the quotation "Better remorse than regret"? Didn't remorse mean being sorry for not taking opportunities when they came? If she let Brad and Thea go without her, wouldn't she feel remorse for missing such an adventure? Surely *that* would be much worse.

Grams, sewing in the lamplight, looked up as Penny came in the door. Penny went over to the stove, lifted the blue spackle coffeepot, and shook it to see if it was still full. She took a mug down from the shelf, poured herself a cup, and brought it over to the table across from where Grams was seated in her rocking chair.

Stirring sugar into her cup and said quietly, "I told Todd I was going."

"And I suppose the boy took it hard."

"Yes, ma'am."

"I think he always planned that someday you and him. . . ."

"Yes. I know. And I'm sorry if I've hurt him."

"Well, just so you don't regret it when it's too late."

Regret! That word kept cropping up! Why did everyone use it? Wasn't it possible that she would think back on her decision as the best one she had ever made?

However, Penny made no comment. She couldn't share with Grams the *real* reason she couldn't back out now. She was caught between two loyalties. The one that bound her to Thea was strong. Thea needed her in a way Grams never could. Grams was a giver, generously pouring out love, acceptance, support to everyone. Thea was an emotional pauper.

While Penny had received an abundance of love from Grams, Uncle Billy, and a wide assortment of relatives, Thea had grown up in a loveless home. She had once confided to Penny that she could never remember being hugged or told she was loved — until Brad.

When Grams knew about the baby, Penny was sure she would understand and approve of her decision to go west.

She soon kissed Grams good night and went upstairs to her loft. There she took down her Bible from its shelf above her bed and, holding it, knelt down. She wasn't sure what she should pray about, but she was sure God knew what she needed. Thumbing through the pages she found in Exodus 33 the heartfelt plea that spoke to her own situation: "Lord, show me Thy way that I might find favor with Thee. If Thy presence does not go with me do not lead me from here."

Penny got into bed feeling assured that if it wasn't right for her to accompany Brad, Thea, and Belinda something would happen to prevent her going.

She bunched the pillow more comfortably and settled herself for sleep, but she lay awake for a long time. Now that she had told Grams her decision, Penny's imagination ran free. Ever since the whole idea of going west had taken hold, she had felt a stirring excitement. That's why the word "regret" fell on deaf ears. Instead she had the strongest feeling that what lay ahead was better than what she was leaving behind. Maybe the unknown promise beyond Dunwoodie, where all her tomorrows waited, was something splendid.

Chapter 6

In the weeks that followed, preparations for the westward journey got underway. The first order of business was the building of the wagon in which they would travel. Brad had secured plans for the commonest type of conveyance, strong and sturdy enough to withstand months of rough terrain. These vehicles were called "prairie schooners" because of their shape, and it took only a little imagination to concede they *did* resemble a sailing ship. Built of oak, the rectangular bed of the wagon was approximately four feet wide and about twelve feet long. A sturdy tool chest was built at one end. The wheels were iron-rimmed wood. The axle assemblies were built with special care and strength, because the probability of the "emigrants" reaching their destination, over plains, deserts, and mountains, depended on its durability and safety. After yards of sturdy canvas cotton were stretched over the bent hickory supports arched from one side to the other, they were then painted with several coats of linseed oil to make them waterproof.

All along both interior sides extra pockets and slings were sewn to provide more storage space. It was easy to see that the interior of the wagon, which served as the travelers' living space, would be cramped.

Penny felt a little awkward when she found out Todd was helping Brad to build it, working nights and every weekend in Brad's barn. She told herself it was only natural that Brad ask for his help or for Todd to offer. After all, they had been friends since boyhood. Penny tried not to see the mournful glances he cast her way when she looked in on their progress, but since she could not avoid him, she did her best to act casual and friendly around him.

Penny knew her decision to go west had become the subject of gossip. Dunwoodie, like most small towns, had no secrets. Talk had come back to her that people wondered how she could go off to California and turn her back on a potential husband as nice as Todd.

But Penny was independent enough to feel she did not have to explain or apologize to anyone. Let them buzz all they wanted. On the whole, she herself never paid much attention to gossip. However, she was secretly glad to learn that Jeremiah had left town to travel with Brother Carmichael. By this she assumed that he was genuinely serious about his own "calling." Well, it didn't concern her and it certainly didn't *include* her. Penny pushed aside her disturbing thoughts about him. Gradually the frightening encounter in the woods and his bizarre proposal faded in the busy preparations for the long journey.

Once the wagon was built, the packing began in earnest. Loading, shifting, and rearranging began. Almost every day, more "necessities" were decided upon, and the whole process had to be gone through again. Bedding and tent supplies, blankets, feather bed, pillows, tent, poles, stakes, ropes, and cooking utensils, Dutch oven, kettle, skillet, coffee grinder and pot, knives, tableware, precious matches placed in a glass jar — all had to be accessible for each night's camp on the trail. Places had to be found for their food provisions — stores of flour, baking soda, coffee, cornmeal, dried meats, vegetables and fruit, molasses, vinegar, pepper, salt, sugar, rice, and tea — which would have to last either the whole two thousand miles or until they reached a settlement where they could be replenished. They had to be very selective in taking Grams' wonderful home-canned delicacies; the glass jars took up too much room and could be broken too easily.

Decisions about clothing were the hardest to make for Penny and Thea. What would life on the trail be like? What might they need when they arrived in California? Daily discussions were held on these weighty matters. Then Brad put his foot down, declaring they each could have only one trunk and Thea would have to share hers with both him and Belinda. That settled, both women packed judiciously, one wool dress apiece. Anticipating it would be the hottest part of summer when they were to cross the prairies, they packed lighter weight gingham dresses. Grams contributed two denim pinafores for each of them, saying, "There'll be lots of dust and dirt to deal with, housekeeping in a traveling wagon." Penny and Thea exchanged a knowing glance, and with a wink and a giggle, each of them packed a party dress — "just in case."

Grams had taken on the job of packing the medicinal supplies. "Young people never think they might get sick. But with a little one along it's best to be prepared," she said as she fitted a small wooden box with some of her own time-tested remedies for stomachache, along with laudanum and camphor for headache, quinine for malaria, hartshorn for snakebite, citric acid for scurvy. . . . " 'Cause, for sure, after a while you'll run out of fresh fruit and vegetables." She gave a definitive nod, then slipped in a large bottle of castor oil and another of peppermint essence.

The three of them spent hours making mattresses to place in the back of the wagon where they'd sleep, and Grams busily finished up an extra quilt to add to the ones already packed. "There'll be plenty of cold nights, I'll be bound, even if you'll be travelin' in summer. I've heard tell even in the Sahara Desert, nights get freezing cold. You'll be glad to have these, more'n likely."

Only a few "luxuries" were permitted. Brad watched doubtfully as Thea lined up the things "she could not bear to part with" to be placed *somewhere* in the wagon. Her mother's set of china, silver teapot, a few books, a Seth Thomas clock with brass trim, and Belinda's cradle. At this, Brad balked.

"We don't need to take *that,* Thea. She's almost outgrown it; she can sleep on a pallet, like the rest of us."

Under Thea's pale skin appeared a blush turning her quite pink. Penny knew Thea was very tempted to tell Brad then that they would certainly *need* that in a few months. There was a moment's hesitation, then Thea said softly, "Please, Brad. My grandfather made it for my mother when she was a baby. I slept in it and Belinda, too — it's a family heirloom."

Penny saw her brother chew his lower lip in frustration; then resignedly he said, "All right, if you insist. But something else'll have to go."

Thea threw a look that said "help" to

Penny, and together they scrambled back into the wagon and started shifting things around again. Thea's gaze landed on a box containing some embroidered linens and pillow slips. Thea pointed at it. Penny knew that Thea had carefully packed her wedding bonnet in among them so that it wouldn't be crushed. She knew how much sentimental value Thea attached to it. It was a symbol of so much — but she also realized the cradle meant more. It would be for the new baby, to be born in the new country for which they were heading, in the new life to which they were going.

By the first week in April everything was packed. The wagon was finished, loaded, and ready to go. The day of their departure for Independence was set.

During that last week before they were to leave, Penny awoke every morning with a funny little feeling in her stomach. Though she had been counting the days, marking them off on the Farmer's Almanac calendar, now that she was about to leave, each day brought a special awareness. Things she had taken for granted, hardly noticed — the first signs of spring, the first green leaves, the bulbs beginning to poke through the ground, the first robin — took on a new significance. Next spring she would be in *California* seeing all kinds of new things.

Though she felt a happy excitement, there was also a melancholy about these last days. Penny found she could not glance at Grams without tearing up. One morning Penny came downstairs, paused on the stairway, and, looking into the kitchen, saw her grandmother moving briskly about fixing breakfast. Penny marveled at the small, straight body, her quick, deft movements. At an age that is considered to be elderly, Grams was as spry as ever.

Penny felt a sharp clutching sensation in her heart. Grams seemed dearer than ever now that she was leaving her. They had both been so busy this past week, there hadn't been a spare minute or an idle hour to talk, to tell her all the things she wanted to say. Penny wondered if that hadn't been her grandmother's purpose, keeping so busy that she wouldn't think too much about them leaving. She knew it would be particularly hard for her to say good-bye to Belinda, who was Grams' special "pet."

There were so many things Penny wanted to tell Grams if only she had a chance: how much she loved her, how much she appreciated all the years of devoted care. Especially she wanted her to know what her unselfishly "freeing" her to go with Brad and Thea meant, not making her feel the least guilty about leaving. This evening, for sure, Penny would say all those things that until now had been in her heart.

When Penny returned from taking a few last-minute things to be placed in her space of the wagon, Grams was sitting in her rocker working on her patchwork. She looked up when Penny came in. "You know, I've been thinking that it'll be some time 'fore you can get to a post office and send a letter back to me. So I want you to keep a journal, Penny. Write something down every day about where you are, what's goin' on, and what it looks like out there." Here she turned her head, looking out the window so Penny couldn't see her suddenly bright eyes. "I reckon you'll see sights that'll be beyond description, but I want you to try to write it all down as best you can. Then when you get to California, you can send it back to me. That way when I read it, it'll be like I was with you all that way."

Impulsively Penny went over and hugged her. "Oh, Grams, I wish you were going with us. Won't you change your mind and come? There's room."

"Land sakes, child, no! Mercy! I can't leave Uncle Billy, and Sister Dora's been hinting she'd like to spend some time over here . . . now that Clem's married. . . . I don't think she likes her daughter-in-law much, and I told

81

her once you all were on your way . . . I'd enjoy the company."

Penny only half believed her. She knew Grams was being brave, putting up a courageous front. It must be very hard to part with the two people she had raised as her own children, to say nothing of Thea and Belinda.

She studied her grandmother's face she knew so well. There were still traces of the young woman that the old daguerreotypes proved had once been Cordelia Sayres. Her silver hair had dark streaks that hinted of lustrous color. But more than past beauty were the lines that life had etched on her face. The happiness, sorrow, wisdom had all left their mark, and it was a lovely legacy.

One of the many things Penny's grandmother had taught her by example was the ability to accept any circumstance, that life itself had something to teach, that you did the task that lay immediately at hand, and trusted God for the rest. Penny had never heard Grams complain, no matter how difficult things seemed. It was an important lesson. Even though Penny admired that quality in her grandmother she had no idea how valuable it would become to her in the days, weeks, and months that lay ahead of her.

PART 2

The Adventure Begins

Chapter 7

At last it came! The day they were to start for Independence. There they would join the other wagons setting out on the Oregon Trail. Brad had made arrangements with a Captain Harding, a veteran of many cross-country treks, to join a train of twenty-five wagons he was leading to the coast, scheduled to depart on the fifteenth of April.

That morning Penny and Grams breakfasted alone early. Later Brad would arrive, driving the wagon with a brace of four oxen, two saddle horses, and their cow, tied to the back end. Then there would be the final farewell. Penny was sure her face must show some of her tension and anxiety about leaving.

As if reading her thoughts, Grams said, "Now, no last-minute nonsense, young lady. You're doing the right thing, Penny. Even though she didn't say anything to me direct, I expect Thea's going to need a sight more than company on this trip."

Penny darted Grams a sharp glance. Had she guessed about the new baby? Although both girls had been careful not to let anything slip, nothing much escaped Grams. But she didn't let on, if she did.

"And you won't forget about keeping a letter-journal, will you?"

"No, ma'am." Penny could hardly speak over the lump rising in her throat, realizing that this was the last time she'd be sitting across the table from her grandmother for a long, long time.

When Brad showed up, Grams bustled about, directing the loading of Penny's belongings, with an extra basket of food she had filled for them. Then followed a great deal of confusion, as other relatives, neighbors, and friends began to gather to see them off. Belinda was handed around to be kissed and hugged by all, and Brad had to listen to Uncle Billy's instructions and Aunt Dora's warnings about trusting strangers. Grams drew Penny aside and whispered, "We'll say our good-bye in here, not in front of the others. Don't want to make a spectacle of myself." She sniffed, then said sternly, "Nor do I want you blubbering, missy!" She gave Penny a hard hug.

Held tight in the arms that had rocked, comforted, and consoled her all the years of her life, Penny held her tight, loath to let go or move out of the embrace.

It was Grams who pulled away first, at the sound of footsteps on the porch and Brad's voice calling out, "All set, Penny? We're ready to roll."

They hurried out and Penny climbed into the wagon from the back. Brad cracked his long-handled whip, and with a neck-jolting jerk, the wagon lurched forward amid the yells and shouts of good-byes.

Penny leaned out as far as she dared, waving frantically. Grams was on the porch waving something in her hand. It looked like a dishtowel. The last thing she saw was that white cloth flapping before they rounded the bend at the end of the road.

Thea was sitting up front on the driver's seat with Brad, holding Belinda on her lap. Since there was no one to see, Penny let the tears come and roll down her cheeks unchecked. For a few awful minutes Penny had the nightmarish feeling that maybe it was an awful mistake to leave her childhood home, all those dear to her, even Todd Farnum, a good man who loved her. . . .

As they rolled through the town where she had grown up, passing all the places she had passed hundreds of times on her way to school or to the church or to the store all these years, mixed with the nostalgia, Penny felt a ripple of excitement. Soon she would be seeing another landscape, another part of the world.

She was, after all, on the brink of the greatest adventure of her life, where anything could happen, where anything was possible. She might even find love — stronger, richer, deeper than she had ever imagined — waiting for her beyond the prairies, over the mountains. They were going to travel into a strange new land. . . .

She took out a newly sharpened pencil and the notebook Grams had given her and balanced it on her lap. Opening it to the first page, she wrote, "The sun is shining, the air is April fresh, and we are on our way. California Ho!"

Then an old thought occurred to her that she had not dared share with anyone: Would she find a love, stronger, richer, deeper than any she had ever imagined or known? Maybe it was only a foolish, romantic dream, but where she was going, she just might find it.

Chapter 8

Independence was congested, its streets jammed with wagons, carts, and jostling crowds of men, mules, and horses. The noise was deafening: merchants hawking their wares to the westward-bound "emigrants" — what they declared were the "necessities" for the long journey. The ring of blacksmithing shops was constant. Long lines of people stood waiting their turn to get their horses and oxen shod. The banging, hammering, braying, and shouting was mixed with hundreds of discordant voices rising to make themselves heard over the constant din.

As Brad maneuvered their wagon and team through the crowded thoroughfare, Thea and Penny, holding Belinda, peeked out from the protection of the canvas curtains. They exchanged horrified glances as they took in the scene. Were all these people on their way to California too? Were they all trying to escape from wherever their homes to find a better life in the "promised land"? They exchanged expressions of thankfulness that they had stocked their wagon with supplies before arriving in Independence. At least they wouldn't have to stop to wait in endless queues to purchase them. Brad finally managed to get them out of the center of town and onto a less crowded road.

From there they would go to a place called Maple Grove, the rendezvous point. Here they would join other westward-bound wagons and meet the wagon master, Captain Harding. Once everyone who had signed up for this train was assembled, the men, the heads of each family, would gather for an organizational meeting. At that time guidelines for the journey would be explained: what routes the train members would take, the daily schedule they would travel by, the routine that they would follow, the rules they would obey. Brad admitted there were quite a few details he didn't fully know, and he admitted he had a good deal yet to learn about this venture and so he looked forward to meeting with the other journeyers.

They were all really eager now. Penny had come up to the front of the wagon, stepping over boxes, rolled up mattresses, quilts, and trunks to crouch behind the other three on the driver's seat. They couldn't stop talking. Here at last was the "jumping-off" place of their journey, the gateway to the exciting new life ahead. Suddenly Brad pulled on the reins to bring the wagon to a stop.

"This must be where we turn," he said, pointing to a crudely printed sign on a rough wooden board nailed to a tree, a painted arrow under the words Maple Grove.

Penny thrust her head between her brother and Thea to see. It didn't look much like a grove. There wasn't a maple tree in sight. It was just a large open space in the middle of an overgrown meadow. They made the turn and slowly went forward. Soon they saw three or four wagons scattered over a wide area. A few horses grazed on the scraggly grass that edged the rutted center. A small group of men huddled to one side and looked around indifferently as Brad drove the wagon into an empty space. For a full minute they all sat there, stunned. Where was the large gathering of wagons ready to go west? At length Brad said, "I'll go see what's goin' on."

Penny sensed that he was trying to sound matter-of-fact, but she guessed he was just as bewildered and disappointed as she and Thea were. The scene before them certainly didn't look like what they had pictured. Nor did the people seem like the band of enthusiastic fellow-adventurers they had anticipated meeting and socializing with and sharing the excitement of the journey with.

Neither Thea nor Penny voiced their apprehension. They remained quiet as they watched Brad, hands in his pockets, assuming a nonchalance they were sure he didn't feel. He ambled up to the small cluster of men, who regarded him curiously.

Belinda, who had fallen asleep with the rocking motion of the wagon, stirred and awakened. "I hungwy."

"In a minute, honey. Let's wait and see what Daddy finds out. Then we'll find a nice place and have supper." Thea soothed her, but her tone did not evidence much hope of finding the "nice place" she promised.

"Do you think one of those men is Captain Harding?" Penny asked.

"I don't know. I sure thought there'd be more people than this, didn't you?"

"Brad said there'd be at least twenty-five or thirty wagons all together. They won't start west with fewer than twenty . . . not safe because of Indians, I guess."

Thea gave a little shudder, and Penny wished she hadn't mentioned Indians. That was one of the hazards of the westward journey that the "emigrants" most feared. She remembered Brother Carmichael calling them "wild savages" that needed to be "tamed." She quickly tried to undo whatever mischief she'd caused by bringing up the subject.

"Of course they're mostly exaggerated —

Indian attacks." She was quick to add, "It's those made-up Wild West stories. Actually, from what I've read most of the Indians are peaceable, just want to trade. That's why we brought all that extra stuff, the calico, combs, trinkets. Remember? That information was in some of the information Brad got when he wrote to Captain Harding. And certainly *he* ought to know. He's led eight wagon trains, it said."

Thea only nodded. Penny hoped that she had allayed her sister-in-law's worries. She wondered just *how* afraid Thea *was* about this whole venture. Thea hadn't talked much about it. The most emotion she'd shown was relief and gratitude once Penny had agreed to come along. She glanced at her sister-in-law with new respect. Hadn't she read some-where that real courage was when you *were* afraid of something, but did the thing you feared anyway?

Penny felt Thea had hidden her fears be-cause of Brad. Few people could resist Brad's persuasive ways. Penny remembered times when he was a little boy wheedling for an ex-tra piece of pie or cake so that even Grams found him irresistible. And she'd never seen Thea disagree with him about anything. But if she really was afraid and didn't want to make this journey — maybe, it would have been better if *this* time Thea had dug in her heels and said no. Even let him go it alone. But of course, Thea would never have done *that!*

Before Penny's thoughts could go any further down this dangerous path, Brad returned. Penny suspected the grin on his face was planted to offset any misgivings the two women might have.

"It's all right," he told them with heartiness. "It'll be another day or so before Captain Harding gets here, as well as everyone else who's signed up. They're coming from all over — Maine, Mississippi, as well as Missouri. We're lucky we got here early and can have our pick of a spot to park our wagon, let the oxen and horses feed . . . pitch a tent." He glanced at Thea. "Now don't look that way, Thea. It's going to be fine. Everything's going to work out."

Penny hoped Brad was right. Anyway, she made up her mind to help him bolster Thea's obvious flagging spirits. She was just tired. The day-long trip in the unaccustomed wagon had been tiring, and Belinda was fretful. She'd be all right once they had eaten.

Determined to be cheerful, Penny got busy helping Thea spread out a blanket on which to set Belinda down. She got out the picnic basket Grams had handed them before they took off and opened it. Just as she had hoped she would she found something to give the child to nibble on until they were able to fix a real supper. Inside were all manner of goodies: blueberry muffins, oatmeal cookies, apples, homemade bread, sliced ham, cold fried chicken, a mound of sweet butter wrapped in cheesecloth. Penny sent up a silent prayer of thanksgiving! What a blessed grandmother they had.

After two long, tedious days Captain Harding still hadn't shown up. Penny kept telling herself it would all come all right. Two or three more wagons pulled into camp, and their occupants would ask the same questions they had asked when they arrived. Nobody seemed to know for sure when the wagon master would come, when the organizing meeting would take place, and, most of all, when they could start west. Some of the men were getting restive. Some even talked of pulling out and joining up with another wagon train. But all it amounted to was talk.

Little by little, some of the women made friendly overtures to Thea. Belinda was such a pretty baby, she always drew people's comments and was clucked over. The women largely ignored Penny. But she was used to being ignored around Thea. All their growing-up years, especially when boys began to take an interest in the opposite sex, Penny had been mainly known for having a "beautiful friend." Boys who had been hers and Brad's playmates for years suddenly hung around, hoping for a chance to be noticed by Thea. Of course Thea only had eyes for Brad, who had taken a long time noticing his little sister's best friend.

But this time, being ignored was different. Penny finally understood why she was being left out of conversations and not sought out. It dawned on her that it was because she was *unmarried* — the *only* unmarried woman in the group thus far. Maybe they regarded her as a threat? How silly! She certainly had no designs on *any* of their husbands. She decided she wasn't going to let it bother her, although it did make her feel a bit awkward.

Brad was getting irritable and restless with the delay. Then on the third day, as if by magic, a group of ten, then another fifteen wagons pulled into Maple Grove. The already assembled bunch greeted them with shouts and cheers. Now it began to look like a real wagon train, and spirits rose. Everyone grew more lively, optimistic, and cheerful.

As every few hours a new wagon filled with other eager "emigrants" pulled into the Maple Grove clearing, good feelings became contagious. Some particularly elated folks painted signs on their canvas tops, with sayings like, "California, Here We Come!" Finally Captain Harding arrived, and the collective sigh of relief was almost audible. Now things would *really* get underway, and they would soon be heading out onto the Oregon Trail.

An organizational meeting was scheduled for that evening, and Brad said they'd have to have an early supper so he could attend. All afternoon the whole camp buzzed with supposition of who would be voted spokesman for the group, the one to whom people could go when they had a problem or a dispute to settle. The rumor was that the men would draw up and agree upon a code of general regulations for the order and mutual protection of the whole train. Each family was independent, providing for their own food and welfare, but every man was expected to do his share of general work: guard duty and livestock picket assignments.

It all sounded splendid to Penny. Penny secretly hoped Brad would be chosen as spokesman. She was proud that Brad already seemed to be well regarded by the other men. Not only was he personable, outgoing, and smart, but he was also generous in offering help to others. His carpentry skills were in particular demand. He readily lent a hand in

97

helping to pitch tents, tend livestock, and drive oxen. There were a surprising number of men who seemed to be lacking in necessary tasks of camping and wagon train living: storekeepers, owners of small businesses, a schoolmaster, and a law clerk were among some of the most eager, enthusiastic would-be western travelers. Penny wondered how a wife felt knowing her husband's obvious inexperience and ineptness as they ventured out on the long journey over plains and mountains, with homesteading and farming as their end goal.

Well, that was one thing about being single. She had no one to worry about but herself. Already she was getting the hang of outdoor living and leading a "tinkers-style life," and she loved every minute of it.

All afternoon a festive air continued to circulate among the camped wagons. Their once flagging spirits were revived by the presence of Captain Harding and the promise of an imminent departure.

Just before they were to prepare Brad's early dinner, Penny and Thea were sitting on the back of the wagon, waiting for Brad to return from taking the oxen for water. They were greeted by a cheerful voice: "Howdy, young ladies."

They turned to see a large gray-haired woman approaching. Smiling, she held out a dish covered with a blue checkered napkin and said, "Just thought you all might enjoy one of my apple pies."

Thea was holding Belinda in her lap, so Penny hopped down and accepted the unexpected but welcome gift. "Why, thank you," Penny said, holding out her hands for the plate.

This was the first open gesture of friendship they'd experienced since they'd pulled into Maple Grove. Each wagon load of travelers seemed to keep to itself as if everyone were waiting for everyone else to make the first move. From Brad, who had been around talking to the other men, they heard that several of the wagons were made up of two or three related families all moving west together. These groups had plenty of company among themselves and were either too shy or too cliquish to extend the circle. But this woman seemed ready not only to be neighborly, but to tell them about herself and to get to know them.

"I'm Nelldean Hardison," the woman said, her weathered face wrinkling in a wide smile. "Me and my grandson Nate's making this trek together. You two sisters?"

"Sisters-in-law. I'm Penny Sayres, and this is my brother Brad's wife, Thea."

"And who's this little sweetie?" Nelldean asked, holding out a finger for Belinda to grasp. Belinda dimpled and held out a chubby hand.

"Belinda." Thea smiled proudly.

"My, ain't she a picture?" Nelldean beamed. "So you're ho for California? Nate and me'll be partin' ways at Fort Hall. We're set for Oregon. Goin' to homestead there. Folks think I'm pretty old to be settin' out for a new country, but I say it's never too late." She chuckled merrily and went on without being prompted. "He's all alone in the world now 'cept for me. My son and daughter-in-law, his ma and pa, went out to Oregon two years ago. Nate was supposed to go with them but got the typhoid, near lost him, but we pulled him through. He was too puny to go with his folks, so he stayed with me until they got settled. They sent us the money to get the equipment we needed to outfit our wagon, and we started planning this here trip. Well, that was over a year ago, and just as we wuz about to leave, we got word both his folks had got sick real sudden and —," Nelldean snapped her fingers "— just like that they wuz both gone to glory." Nelldean sighed. "But we'd bought the wagon and had it fitted out, and Nate was rarin' to go, so anyway, well, I couldn't let him go by hisself now could I?

He's got a homestead waitin' in Oregon, so that's where we're plannin' to settle. So how about you folks? Going to California to mine or to homestead?"

"Homestead," Penny replied. "At least Brad and Thea are; I'm just along for the ride. I'll be going back once they're settled."

Nelldean gave her a skeptical glance but didn't say anything. They chatted a few more minutes, then Brad came back tired and ready for a supper they hadn't yet started. Penny introduced him to Nelldean, who shook his hand and said, "Well, I'll be goin' and let you folks get your supper." When they thanked her again for the pie, she waved her hands dismissively. "Jest hope you all enjoy it. I believe in bein' neighborly. Even when we're all on the move. Never know when you might need a helpin' hand, and it's nice to know the folks you're travelin' with. I'll bring Nate by so's you can get acquainted with him too." She nodded to Brad. "Good for a boy to have an older man he can look up to and kinda ask for advice he might not want to ask his old gramma for!" She chuckled and went on back to the wagon parked up away from theirs.

Penny and Thea worked together to get their belongings ready. The fact that this meant they were really going to get started on their great adventure made for a lightheartedness in contrast to the worry of the last few days. The two women went about setting things out on the small makeshift table, joking and laughing. Watching them Belinda clapped her tiny hands and laughed along with them. This made them laugh all the more. The result of all this merriment was a meal more like a carefree picnic.

An hour or so before Brad was to attend the men's meeting, Penny and Thea got out the makeshift table of small, square boards nailed together, and they set out their supper. Thanks to Grams, they had another bounteous meal — sliced ham, homemade bread, quince jam — and they opened a jar of Bartlett pears. Belinda seemed happy as a little gypsy, sitting on the ground and eating with both dimpled hands. Every so often she crowed with delight. Thea and Penny alternated between excitement and silliness. The least little thing sent them into hilarious giggles.

Nelldean's pie was delicious — better than either of them could make, Brad teased them. "I encourage you two to keep up *that friendship*." More than the treat of the pie, Penny appreciated Nelldean's obvious generous nature. It gave her a sense of security to know that there was an older woman who had raised a family of her own, suffered the ups and downs of life, and had a wealth of experience and knowledge that neither she nor Thea possessed. As the jovial woman had said, you never knew when you might need a neighbor. Certainly there were unknown hazards in this moving caravan of people on this uncharted journey west. It was good to know Nelldean Hardison was on their wagon train.

After supper Brad walked over to the organizational meeting with some of the other men, and Thea took Belinda inside the wagon to put her down for sleep. Left to herself, Penny leaned against the wagon and looked up at the sky. It was just beginning to get dark. A few tiny stars began to appear, and the pale line of a new moon etched itself against the gray-mauve background.

Just then she heard the creaking sound of yet another wagon turning into the campground, its humped outline rocking as it moved awkwardly forward over the rutted surface of the ground. The driver was obviously searching for a place to camp.

A man and woman sat on the high driver's seat. Slowly the wagon advanced, then pulled to a stop directly in front of where Penny stood. The man turned his head so that Penny saw his face clearly. For a moment all she could do was stare, horrified. Then she drew in her breath sharply. "Oh, no!" The man was none other than Jeremiah Bradshaw.

Chapter 9

Penny's first horrified reaction was to duck out of sight. Not wanting him to see *her*, she crouched behind the wagon, her heart pounding. Jeremiah Bradshaw! Of all people she had never expected to see — never *wanted* to see! If she imagined the worst possible thing that could happen to her, it would be to have him on the same wagon train.

How had it happened? He had left Dunwoodie to travel with Brother Carmichael before she had decided to go with Brad and Thea. She had been so glad not to have to see or talk to him — to have him out of her life! Now, here he was back in it.

Gradually Penny collected her wits. His wagon passed theirs. Sure that he had not seen her, she crept from her hiding place, watching as his wagon went toward the center of the campground where the large campfire was burning. Most of the menfolk were gathered there at the organizational meeting, and Captain Harding would be there to greet the newcomers.

Who was the woman with Jeremiah? His

wife? It *must be.* It certainly wasn't his mother, and he didn't have a sister. When had Jeremiah married? And *who* was she?

After Jeremiah's wagon passed by, Penny climbed into the wagon. As she did Thea looked up. She was just covering Belinda, and she put a finger to her lips, warning her to be quiet so as not to wake up Belinda. Something in Penny's expression alarmed Thea, and she crawled over to where Penny huddled at the edge of the wagon and whispered, "What ever's wrong?"

"You'll never guess." Penny shivered and told Thea what she had seen. In hushed tones she said, "How can I possibly avoid him if they're going to be traveling with us?"

"I don't know." Thea looked forlorn. "Poor Penny. I know you couldn't stand him. None of us could figure out exactly why —"

Involuntarily Penny shuddered, remembering the effect Jeremiah's unwanted attention had on her. "I can't explain it. He's just so — so —" She shook her head.

Thea patted her shoulder sympathetically. "Don't bother. I understand. I'll try to find out more about them tomorrow. I'll ask some of the women — without mentioning you, of course. I've been talking to some of them, the ones with small children. Mothers always talk to each other. About their little ones — how old are they, when did they start to talk or walk, that sort of thing."

Penny knew Thea was being tactful. *She* had been more or less ignored by the other women. Be that as it may, she'd let Thea do her detective work about the Bradshaws.

Actually it was Brad who brought back the information they had been curious about. He shared the news that he had been temporarily voted spokesman for their group of wagons, but it was his other bit of news that interested Penny personally. "Say, Penny, an old beau of yours just turned up to be part of our wagon train. Jeremiah Bradshaw. He's got a wife with him though, so I guess his heart wasn't broke too long," he told her teasingly.

"He was no beau of mine!" Penny declared indignantly. "What did he have to say?"

"He seemed mighty surprised to find out you'd come along with Thea and me."

Penny and Thea exchanged looks.

"What *exactly* did he say about me?" Penny asked.

"Oh, just something about you always were a will-o'-the-wisp." Brad shrugged. "We didn't talk much. He sat in on the meeting and made a few suggestions. Which weren't well taken, I must say, as he had just arrived on the scene and didn't know anyone. Seemed kinda pushy."

"You said his wife is with him. Is she from Dunwoodie too?" asked Thea.

"No, funny thing. Brother Carmichael — you remember him? — well, seems like he had been to this woman's town and convinced *her* that she too was to go west as a missionary, then introduced her to Jeremiah and married them."

Penny would have liked more details about this startling occurrence, but Brad yawned and said he was going to "hit the hay." "Coming, Thea?" He held out his hand to her, and she took it and, with an apologetic look back at Penny, went along with him into the wagon.

Penny stayed by the campfire a little longer, knowing that sleep would not come easily for her this night. What would having Jeremiah in such proximity for the next several months be like? She couldn't bear the thought. She knew one day soon the encounter she dreaded would have to happen — was bound to happen. She doubted if he would create a scene as long as she was under Brad's protection. Still, a cold shudder went through her. All the joy and excitement she had felt about the trip drained away. The menacing figure of Jeremiah loomed over her like a giant shadow.

Only a few nights later Penny came face-to-face with Jeremiah. Thankfully, she was with

Thea and Brad. The whole company had been called to a final meeting before getting under way the following day, to receive last minute instructions on the order in which each wagon would pull out and in what sequence. Their eyes had met for one terrible moment. The saying "If looks could kill . . ." flashed through Penny's mind. Quickly she averted her head as though listening intently to what the wagon master was saying. When the meeting was over, Jeremiah and his wife had disappeared. Still, Penny was glad she had not been alone this first time he had seen her.

PART 3

On the Trail

Chapter 10

There were thirty wagons in their train now and so much for each group to do every day that Penny assured herself there was little chance of her having to deal with Jeremiah. Even less when the wagons were lined up in the order of their arrival so that when they finally pulled out, the Sayres' was near the front, while the Bradshaws', among the last to join the train, was at the end. When the wagons circled at sunset, they were camped a long way from Jeremiah and his wife.

At the few glimpses she had of Emily Bradshaw, a slight, pale girl with light brown hair and large, frightened eyes, Penny's soft heart felt a nudge of sympathy. She looked sad, anxious, as though she were longing for a kind word, a show of friendship from some of the other women, but too shy to make any gestures herself. Most were too busy with their own chores and children. Even moved by pity, Penny knew *she,* of all the women, could not take any step toward friendship. Whatever she did would be wrongly construed.

For the most part, Penny tried to forget that Jeremiah was in the wagon train and live her own life. She had taken to this unusual way to travel, as Grams would say, "like a duck takes to water." As a child she had often fantasized about the gypsy life, having a little painted caravan, and going wherever the road led. Traveling in the huge canvas covered wagon was far different, but in those first few weeks of the journey Penny enjoyed it thoroughly.

She also tried to keep her promise to Grams of keeping a letter-journal of their days to post at the first mail house or military fort they came to along the trail. She tried to give her grandmother a picture of what life on the trail was like — a life that Penny knew would seem strange to a woman who had lived in the same town all her life and in the same house since she was seventeen!

Life on the trail was so much busier than she had imagined with so many chores to be done — and quickly. In the morning, at the wagon master's shout, they had to be ready to pull their wagon into line in its correct position.

They had been traveling for two weeks before Penny figured out the best time to write to her grandmother: usually the noon break. That was when the wagons pulled off to give the mules, horses, and oxen some rest and for the weary travelers to get a bite to eat. Penny would settle herself at the side of the wagon in the shade, prop her copybook on her knees, and begin to write.

Dearest Grams,

I've tried to jot down something every day that will keep a record of our journey, but I've done a poor job of it so far. But there has been so much to do, so much to see, well — that's my excuse — the days are so full and busy and by nightfall we're all too tired to do much but fix and eat supper, go to bed. I'm still trying to get the hang of this life on the trail. Let me just tell you how it goes.

Morning begins at daybreak. You'd laugh to see me jump when the guard-duty men's rifles go off with a shattering bang. That lets us know we were kept safe and sound through the night by these brave fellas. It's also the signal that we have just two hours to get breakfast, wash up, pack up, and get "ready to roll," as they say around here, before pulling out on the trail for the day's journey. We're supposed to make ten to twelve or more miles per day in order to get to the mountains and cross them before the first snows that sometimes come early in the Sierra.

There's not much chance of sleeping in because there's racket aplenty as folks rouse themselves and get their breakfast going. You never heard such clanging of skillets, banging kettles to say nothing of barking dogs. You'd be surprised how many folks brought their dogs along on this trip. I try to get up first to give Thea time to get the baby up and dressed. I'm getting fairly good at starting a fire. Brad, who was never a morning person, as you may remember, hauls himself out of the wagon, groaning as he gets the team, who aren't that eager either, yoked up. I can sympathize with the poor beasts being hitched for another hard day on the road. We do everything to lighten the load for them. Often Thea and I walk alongside, as do the other women and children. We take turns carrying Belinda who's getting mighty heavy. We've become good friends with a very nice older lady, Nelldean Hardison, who walks with us most days.

Penny paused. She thought of the conversation she'd had with Nelldean the other afternoon when Thea had taken Belinda to the wagon for a nap. Penny always enjoyed Nelldean's company. She was always cheerful and talkative and never complained or whined like some of the women.

Noting that Penny was bareheaded, Nelldean told her, "You've got a fine head of hair, my girl, but what you need is a good sunbonnet, elseways you're going to ruin your complexion and might get sunstroke to boot. I made me a couple 'fore we started out, with broad brims stiffened with narrow wood stays. They'll keep the sun out of your eyes, protect your skin, and keep you from gettin' your brains fried." She chuckled. "I'll make you and your sister ones too. She looks right delicate. Don't see her out walkin'. Is she ailing?"

Penny shook her head, wondering if it might not be a good idea to tell Nelldean Thea was expecting, in case — in case, what? That question stopped her. After all, it was Thea's news to tell, and since Brad didn't know yet, Penny felt she better not. Penny simply said, "She's fine; it's easier for her to nap when Belinda does."

Nelldean didn't make any further comment. But it made Penny wonder if she ought to tell Grams. It wouldn't make any difference now for her to know. Still, she hesitated.

Nelldean spoke again. "Women need a lot of strength for this journey. And more when they get where they're going. Homesteading takes all a body's got and more." Penny felt Nelldean's quick, inquisitive glance. "Did you mean what you said the night I met you? That you're just 'along for the ride?' Why, I'd think a young woman like you'd be up for adventure yourself. I seen you riding your horse the other day, and I said to myself, 'That young lady's going to make a fine homesteader.' "

"Well, you see, I live with my grandmother. She reared Brad and me, and I'll be going back home after I help Thea get settled — well, that's just the way I planned. I only promised Thea I'd stay until —," Penny caught herself before she blurted out Thea's secret.

"I see." Nelldean nodded.

Penny had a feeling the woman guessed what she had not said and in some way it comforted her to know somebody else knew.

Penny went back to her letter-journal. Her pencil skimmed over the pages as she gave her grandmother as vivid a picture as possible of what her far-away family was experiencing. She tried to give her an idea of what a "normal" day on the trail was like for them. She knew it was impossible to describe it to her as it really was, but she tried.

Two hours after sunrise the wagons are

ready to roll. At noon the wagons turn off. The teams are not unyoked but are loosed from the wagons to graze nearby. Sometimes while people eat an "in hand" meal of bread or cheese, the men hold meetings to take care of any business that may need to be discussed or any arguments to be settled. You'll be glad to know Brad is very well regarded among the other men. He's matured a lot and become much steadier and more responsible.

Brad has been voted one of the seven duty captains, whose responsibilities are to assign jobs and oversee some of the wagon repair and other chores on the wagon train. My particular charge is taking care of our two saddle horses, Brad's and mine; Mariah is doing real well. I often put Belinda up in the saddle in front of me and ride. She loves it.

She stopped writing for a minute, pausing to think what to say next. Penny did not know how much to tell of some of the unexpected things that went on: the petty arguments, the problems no one was prepared for, the hardships, and the physical stress of this journey. Much of these were offset by the camaraderie of the other travelers and the congenial companionship the three of them shared. The main thing she didn't tell her grandmother was the arrival of Jeremiah Bradshaw and his wife. It took her only seconds to decide not to say anything. At least not yet. So far, she had managed to keep her distance from both the Bradshaws. She hoped she could maintain that distance all the way to California.

Instead Penny told Grams about the funny things that happened: their new style of cooking over an open fire, the words Belinda was beginning to say, and some of the mishaps of wagon train living.

Penny scribbled busily until she heard the familiar "Wagons! Pull out!" The noon break was over, and they had to start moving again. She quickly put away her notebook and pencil. Once the call was given, everyone hastened to be ready to move out. Over and over they had heard repeated how important it was to make those ten or more miles every day and keep up with the other trains. "A day lost is lost forever." It was necessary to keep the teams of animals in good shape so that there would be no delays. More than once Penny heard Brad repeat what he'd heard the scout and wagon master say: Worst thing you can do is fritter one day on the trail.

All that was necessary to keep the worst laggard moving was to mention the dread words "the Donner Party." Every emigrant knew the tragic story of the members of an earlier wagon who had been caught in a blizzard and were trapped for a horrible winter. There were stories of starvation — or worse.

Tucking her book into one of the pockets of the canvas marked for her belongings, Penny grabbed her new sunbonnet, tied the strings under her chin, and started walking alongside the wagon. "Coming, Thea?" she asked her sister-in-law.

Thea looked up from the pallet on which she was resting beside the sleeping Belinda. "I think I'll stay in for a while. I have a little headache," she said wanly.

Penny started to say something but thought better of it. Just the other evening she had begged Thea to tell Brad. But Thea shook her head, "Not yet, Penny. Just till we get further on our way. I don't want to give him any reason to turn back. I had some of the same queasiness with Belinda; it will pass. I'll just be careful. Please, Penny. Brad is so happy. He's in his element, can't you see that? We can't spoil it for him."

The pleading in Thea's beautiful eyes was impossible to refuse. Penny jumped off the back of the wagon, and as Brad cracked his whip and the wagon made a jolting start, she fell into step alongside.

Lately Thea had been staying in the wagon more than walking, and Penny was worried. Two other women in their company were also expecting, sooner than Thea, however, from what Penny could tell. She would have to be more aware of Thea's condition and take over some of the heavier chores, like lifting and carrying Belinda or placing her in front of her on her saddle when Penny rode Mariah.

Penny did not mind walking. It gave her time to think. She still wondered what it would be like when they reached California, still miles and months away, and how long she would stay. At least until Thea had the baby. Then she would return home. Would that be as hard to do as it had been to come? She could not help wondering if it would be the golden land of promise it had been portrayed as being.

Preoccupied with her own thoughts, time passed quickly for Penny, and soon the signal was given for the wagons to pull out at the end of the day. Penny followed along as Brad guided the oxen into their place in the circle that the wagons always formed for the night for protection from any possible attack by hostile Indians. Thank God, so far there had been none.

At the end of the long day everyone felt relief. This journey was far harder than anyone had anticipated, for both humans and animals. While the men unhitched the teams, the women greeted each other and stood chatting for a few minutes, and the freed children ran around playing tag with friends from some of the other wagons.

Penny and Thea got busy preparing the evening meal. At supper there generally wasn't too much talking; they were all too tired. Gradually things quieted, voices got lower, the night guards left to take their places, beds were unrolled, and children were hushed and readied for sleep. Brad soon left them to crawl wearily into the wagon to sleep. Belinda usually fell asleep in Thea's arms and she took her inside. Penny always insisted on cleaning up and dousing the fire before climbing into her blanket roll. Brad had helped her pitch her small tent at the back of the wagon, not too far from where both horses were tethered for the night. She liked hearing their soft whinnying, the movement of their hooves on the grass, and she liked being able to look out through the flap at the sky. As they reached the prairies the sky seemed bigger than ever. Tonight it was pinpricked with brilliant stars.

Penny, even though tired, didn't usually go right to sleep; her mind always seemed too busy. There was so much to see and learn as they traveled westward. She lay there listening as the night deepened, and a restful silence hovered, then gradually settled over the campground. On nights like this she was glad she'd been persuaded to come along on this journey. Finally her eyelids grew heavy, and Penny drifted slowly off, thinking, *I wouldn't have missed this for the world.*

Chapter 11

For the most part, Penny's daily entries into her letter-journal to Grams were full of the funny incidents and the things she noticed about people, events, happenings that would interest her grandmother as she read it.

You probably recall when we went to hear Brother Carmichael, he went on and on so about what coming west would be like — "Friends, you are traveling to the Garden of Eden, a land flowing with milk and honey" — I'm sure there were some who believed every word. I've begun to think it would have been well for some to take all that with your often counseled "grain of salt." I don't know what California will be like exactly, but I doubt "the clover in Oregon grows high as your chin." However, the wildflowers on the prairies we've passed through are the prettiest and most colorful I've ever seen.

We are becoming fast friends with the Hardisons. Hardly a day goes by that there isn't some sort of exchange between our wagons. Nelldean reminds me something of you, Grams, wise and witty and as cheerful as the day is long. Nothing seems to daunt her. She's a treasure trove of information, which is very helpful to us as we make do with the housekeeping chores while being constantly on the go. You see, Nelldean has already made this cross-country trip once. She and her husband came shortly after the discovery of gold, so she knows more what's ahead of us than anyone else. Nelldean's grandson, Nate, a gangly, freckled sixteen-year-old, is shy but just as generous and open-hearted as his grandmother. Belinda adores him, and he's real sweet with her. Of course, it is Belinda who is the center of attention in our small party. I wish you could see her, Grams. She is growing prettier every day, blonde ringlets now curling around her neck, her skin rosy and healthy from being outdoors so much. And with the sweetest, cunningest ways.

Jotting down the simple details of everyday life on the trail, Penny deliberately left out telling her grandmother about Jeremiah Bradshaw's harassing presence.

The fact that in the few weeks since the

Bradshaws had joined the wagon train she had managed to avoid any direct contact with Jeremiah gave Penny a certain complacency. A false sense of security, as it turned out.

One afternoon when Penny was coming back from drawing a bucket of water from the barrel at the rear of the wagon, a tall figure suddenly loomed in front of her. Jeremiah. Instinctively Penny stepped back, heart thundering. Without any greeting, he planted himself in her path. His mouth twisted sardonically. "Well, Miss Sayres, I thought you didn't want to go west," he snarled.

Penny tried to keep her voice even and remain calm. "I hadn't planned to —"

"Don't lie to me. Don't you know falsehood will not go unpunished? And he who speaks lies will not escape but *perish?*"

"I'm not lying," she said coldly.

"What about your grandmother?" he sneered. "You told me you couldn't leave your grandmother. Or was that another lie?"

"Of course not. I wasn't lying. I came because Thea needed me and —"

"So it was just with *me* you didn't want to come?"

Jeremiah's eyes were dilated, his nostrils quivered, a muscle in his cheek twitched. Penny's mouth went dry with fear. She remembered that awful encounter with him in the woods back home, and she shrank from a repetition. Any minute he could lose complete control. There was no use trying to deal with Jeremiah. He only saw things the way he wanted to see them. Just like he had insisted he had a divine word that *they* were to go together as missionaries. She felt the old revulsion of him rise up within her, but she knew better than to enrage him further. All his fury at her rejection of him was more physical than spiritual. He was using her failure to go along with *his* vision as a cover for his crushed pride. Penny prayed frantically for help.

"That was it, wasn't it?" he demanded. "You risked disobeying God because you didn't want me? You think you're too good for me, don't you?"

"I don't owe you any explanation, Jeremiah," Penny said, trying to control her inner trembling. "Now, let me pass —"

"Not yet. Not until I get an answer."

"You had your answer, Jeremiah, back in Dunwoodie."

He shook his head, eyes blazing, his fists clenched. "You're so proud, aren't you, Penny?" He flung the words at her sarcastically. "Well, you know what pride is? One of the deadly sins! And *you'll* see — pride goeth before a fall, Penny. There's retribution for people like *you* —"

126

He's crazy, stark raving mad! Penny thought frantically. *I have to get away from him.* She tried to pass by him, but he grabbed her wrists.

"Let me go!" Angrily, she tried to pull away, but his grip was too strong. Desperately her eyes darted to the left and right, hoping someone would break this up just by walking by! But there was no one. She was wedged between the two wagons, hidden by their height and bulk, shadowed by the fast-falling dusk, and caught here alone with Jeremiah.

His fingers gripped harder, his voice thickened. "You like tormenting me, don't you, Penny?"

"Of course not, Jeremiah. Why should I?"

"Because you know how much I wanted you to be with me, how it grieved me that you wouldn't listen to what I know was meant to be —"

He pulled her to him, one hand roughly forcing her chin up, his mouth coming down bruisingly on hers. Penny dropped the bucket and felt the cold water splash onto her skirt hem and shoes as it fell to the ground. Then she put both hands against Jeremiah's chest, pushing with all her strength. Taken off guard, he staggered back, stumbling. She drew back her hand and slapped his face as hard as she could.

Jeremiah's palm went to the side of his cheek, already turning red from the stinging blow. His expression went from stunned surprise to total blankness. For a second he neither spoke nor moved. Only his burning eyes betrayed his anger.

"You'll regret you did that, Penny."

"And what about *you*, Jeremiah? You're a married man," she retorted in a low, furious voice. Something buried deep in her memory came into her mind. She decided to flog him with his own weapon: Scripture. "Matthew five, twenty-eight! Think about it —"

The brief glimpse Penny had of Jeremiah's face before he swung on his heel and marched away gave her the satisfaction of knowing that her words had hit their mark. As he disappeared from her sight, she shook her hand, her fingers still tingling from the slap. A feeling of weakness swept over her, and she had to lean against the nearest wagon wheel to steady herself. For a wild moment, the urge to laugh almost overcame her. She knew she must be on the edge of hysteria. Slowly a sense of thankfulness followed. A psalm she had memorized as a child came to her in all its beauty and truth. It was Psalm 18:48: "You have delivered me from a violent man, therefore I will give thanks to you — and sing praises to your name." "Thank you, Lord," she whispered. With a grateful heart she blessed Grams for insisting she memorize Bible verses every week.

That night as she lay sleepless in the dark of the little tent Penny had no doubt whatsoever that she had a Father in heaven who was watching over and protecting her.

Shuddering at the memory of that encounter, resolutely Penny determined to push the nasty incident with Jeremiah out of her mind. How dare he use Scripture to twist and distort? How had she caused him to be so vengeful? She hadn't meant to and she was sorry if she had.

Penny pulled the covers up around her chin, trying to banish the hate-filled scene from her mind. But in spite of her resolve, Jeremiah's voice still echoed hauntingly: "Pride goeth before destruction and a haughty spirit before a fall."

Dearest Grams,

Remember the saying that journeying west was "going to see the elephant" — meaning, I guess, that we were bound to see sights we never had before or could imagine? Well, I have yet to see an elephant, but I've just seen my first buffalo! One day a herd came thundering toward us; it looked like a great dark cloud, a moving mountain coming on with terrible speed. I have no idea how many there were — it seemed a monstrous group, making awful noises, hoof beats clattering, wild snorting, heads down, tails flying. It was an awesome sight to behold. When stampeding, they do not swerve to the left or right but go straight ahead, not stopping for anything. Our scout, waving his arms and shouting, rode down the line telling us to move out of the way of this bunch of animals moving ever closer like a marauding army. But some wagons could not pull out soon enough, and two were overturned as the buffalo rushed by. Two buffalo were shot and their carcasses stripped, butchered, and divided among the wagon train. A huge fire was built, and the meat barbecued. At first I was not eager to try it, but persuaded to taste it, I found it richer and gamier than beef steak. Some said the rest would be made into jerky. Not particularly appetizing to me, but perhaps as we go further and food rations get scarcer, anything will taste good.

Sometimes our evenings are quite lively. As a company of fellow travelers we seem to have come together as a constantly moving band of neighbors. After supper, when the evening chores are done, a group of us often gathers around a campfire. One man is a talented guitar player, another accompanies him on his harmonica, playing familiar melodies that we can all join in singing: "Old Kentucky Home," "The Girl I Left Behind Me," "Maryland, My Maryland." But when they swing into "Home Sweet Home," it touches many a pensive heart, and soon there is a chorus begging them to play something more cheerful. Obligingly they go into "O Susannah" or "Turkey in the Straw." But all in all it is as pleasant a time as can be imagined after the long, wearying days.

I have found there are several other unmarried women in our wagon train, all younger than me! At the ripe old age of twenty-one I'm considered a "spinster," I suppose, and so out of the running for the three bachelors among us. One is a law student and can be seen with a thick tome of jurisprudence open, studying it as he walks alongside his team. The other two are taking "absence without leave" from their college education, but one of these is our harmonica player so we are all happy he did so to make our campfires so enjoyable.

So the social life here at the end of the day is remarkably active! Thea has provided me with an interesting — but I must say "creative" — history. She tells people the story of a "broken engagement" that she says I am bravely recovering from — wouldn't Todd be surprised to know he supposedly jilted *me?* Anyway, it seems to have earned the sympathy of some of the women who had been "snubbing" me for being single, and everyone is quite friendly now.

In her letters to her grandmother, however, Penny still left out many of the things she thought might worry her, things that were burned deeply into her own memory. Penny knew she would never forget them. She might even write about them — someday.

They had been a little more than two months on the trail now, and many disasters had struck their wagon train. Some of the livestock had died, some from overwork, some from a mysterious prairie-induced illness. A few wagons had not been well-built and broke down, beyond repair. Those families had to unload, leaving some of their belongings strewn beside the trail, and join with relatives in their already overcrowded wagons. As wagons broke down, more women and children were forced to walk during the day and bed down in camp on blankets on the ground at night because the interiors of the remaining wagons were too full for any kind of comfort or sleep.

There were disputes and conflicts, even fistfights, as tempers grew raw and nerves taut. There was illness. Once a fever or disease hit one group, it seemed to sweep through the entire wagon train. There were hastily dug graves to join the ones they had seen earlier, then averted their eyes from as they moved along. A few of the water barrels, staves swollen from the desert heat, sprung cracks, leaking precious water and causing a rationing of water for both humans and animals. This commodity could not be wasted. They had to hold out until they reached Fort Laramie, where some of the supplies could be replenished. Nelldean told Penny that these things were all things expected to happen on such a long journey and that the wagon train had been fairly lucky thus far with no epidemics like cholera and no Indian attacks. Her comment didn't make things any more bearable, but it reinforced Penny's decision not to pass all this along in her letters to Grams.

The children on the wagon train were the only ones who seemed carefree. Never had they been allowed so much freedom as they had on the trail. However, there had been some accidents. Tragedies. A couple of children had been run over by wagon wheels; another, running along behind, had tried to jump onto the end of the wagon but slipped and was crushed under the oxen-pulled wagon just behind. There had been illness too, sudden unexplained fevers that took one child, who had been running and playing the day before. The child was quickly buried, and the grieving family had to move on.

Jeremiah Bradshaw remained the "fly in the ointment" for Penny. She hated the feeling of looking over her shoulder, so to speak, always dreading another nightmare encounter. She couldn't entirely avoid him. Every so often she'd see him at a distance, and if he was able to catch her eye, there was always a dark, glowering stare. She didn't think he would seek her out again. But there was always that possibility, and that bothered her.

Nelldean and Penny's friendship strength-ened with each passing day. Penny realized she was transferring some of her affection for Grams to this woman, on whom she found herself relying more and more for advice and counsel.

Nelldean's late husband had been in his thirties when gold was discovered in Califor-nia. "We were both young and full of beans," she reminisced. "No hardship seemed too much for us. We was goin' to make our fortune, you see," she chuckled. "But it didn't turn out that way. Johnny didn't strike it rich. He was a farm boy who got carried away with all the tales of how easy it was going to be. We come back and took over his father's farm. We had to stand all those 'I told you so's.' " Nelldean laughed heartily. "But Johnny proved himself a good farmer, and we raised our family. Four boys. Lost two early on, now the other two both gone. That's why coming with Nate was so important for me. And then that boy's got a good head on his shoulders. We're going to homestead, and it'll work. The good Lord willin' *this* time it's all going to turn out just fine."

Nelldean's optimism and faith were inspiring. They gave new strength to Penny's own hope of how it was all going to be once her brother and Thea got to California.

Dearest Grams,

I think yesterday was one of the happiest days we have had on the trail. There's such a feeling of optimism among us all. We're right on schedule, and it looks as though if we keep up the daily mileage our captain has set for the wagon train, we'll reach the mountains in early September, long before any chance of winter snows, which is considered the most dangerous part of the entire trip.

At Soda Springs we camped by the river for a few days, and we had a chance to catch up on our laundry, pick berries, and generally enjoy a welcome respite from the daily grind of endless travel. This is a beautiful spot. Rocky rims glow all around, golden in the sunlight, grassy slopes dotted with cedar trees stretched out in front of them. You've never seen such wildflowers. They seem brighter and more vividly colored than any back home.

But best of all I want to tell you about our "escapade." When Thea and I had finished our washing, we felt pretty proud of what we'd accomplished. Then, I guess, that mischief in me, which you've always known was there, nudged me. The river was shimmering in the sun so invitingly, I simply couldn't resist. I whispered to Thea, "Let's go downstream a little, round that bend, where no one can see us, and go swimming!" Thea looked a little shocked at my suggestion. But not too much so! We gathered up Belinda, took off our shoes and stockings, waded past to where there was a private spot, and we divested ourselves of skirts and petticoats and in our camisoles and pantaloons went into the cool water. After all the days of dusty travel I can't tell you how delicious it felt against our skin. We held Belinda between us, and she had such a time kicking her feet and splashing as we dipped and bobbed, paddling her chubby little feet in the water. We passed Belinda back and forth, taking turns, and we were soon having the time of our life, just like the children we used to be.

By mid-June a change took place that no one had counted on; some thought it was positive, some negative. A wagon train, made up of Iowans, had left Independence less than a week behind theirs and had now caught up with them. They wanted to join the Missourians, which would add about twenty wagons to the train. It seems they'd heard from folks coming back along the trail that there might be Indian trouble ahead. The men whom the Iowans had sent to a joint meeting felt it would be safer to have a bigger train, more men, more guns. If the Missourians agreed, they would need to vote on a new leader for both caravans. Captain Harding called a meeting of the men to hear the Iowans' proposal and vote on whether or not to join the two wagon trains. Right after supper Brad departed to join the circle of other heads of families who were gathering for discussion.

Penny was left alone by the campfire while Thea went into the wagon to put Belinda down for the night. Penny wished the women had some say-so about the matter. She had her own reservations about joining up with the Iowa wagon train. From the little she had observed while they had all been camped by the river, the Iowa emigrants had little in common with the Missourians. In fact, the two camps, waiting to start on the trail, couldn't have been more different. The Iowans deemed it all right to work on Sunday if they were to be ready to leave the first of the week, but the Missourians strictly observed the Sabbath and did nothing, which made them have to scramble to get all the chores done, everything in readiness for the dawn departure.

Penny just had an uneasiness about joining forces. If an Iowan was voted leader, for instance, would the Missourians get a fair hearing if any disputes arose? She had felt far safer with the slow-speaking Alvin Wright, whom they had voted to be their trail leader before leaving Independence.

She didn't share her misgivings with her sister-in-law when Thea rejoined her at the campfire. But she was eager to know the outcome when Brad returned from the meeting. He seemed in a thoughtful mood.

"So what was decided?" she asked.

"We decided to think it over and then come together again tomorrow night and vote on it."

"Do you think it's a good idea?" Penny persisted.

"I'm not sure. Of course, they've got a point — I mean, *if* there *are* hostile Indians ahead, the more, the better. . . ."

Thea moved closer to Brad, who put a protective arm around her shoulders.

In her tent that night, Penny hoped her doubts about the wisdom of joining the two wagon trains were unfounded. After all they had almost two thousand more miles to travel before reaching California, and what lay ahead no one could be sure. Maybe Brad was right, the more men and guns, the less danger.

But the next evening when Penny went to fetch their water, she overheard something that did nothing to reassure her. Moving between two parked wagons, with two heavy water buckets, Penny stopped to catch her breath for a minute before shifting them from one hand to the other. That's how she happened to overhear two men talking. She hadn't meant to eavesdrop, but they made no effort to lower their voices. They were discussing the proposed meeting of both wagon trains for the evening clearly. Even before their voices dropped, she overheard part of their conversation: "Most of them Missourians aren't dry behind the ears yet. A bunch of farmers, don't know nuthin' about what's in store on the trail."

"Takin' a full day off on Sundays — lot of nonsense, if you ask me."

"Once I'm in charge there ain't goin' be no pampering, let me tell you. We gotta git through those mountains before winter. If they can't keep up, we'll just leave them greenhorns."

"Well, let's be sure we got a majority. Even if it takes some arm twistin'."

There was a rumble of laughter, then the other voice said, "And majority goes."

The tone of their voices and what she'd overheard didn't bode well for the Missourians. Should she warn Brad, tell him what she'd overheard? But there wasn't a chance. When she got back to the wagon two other men were waiting for her brother while he ate a plate of beans and biscuits, then they all hurried off to the meeting. She just had to hope it would all work out for the best.

It was late when Brad returned. Penny and

Thea had waited up, anxious to know what had been decided. He told them Iowan Thomas Meecham had been elected leader.

"By a majority," Brad told them adding cynically. "Seems like he spent most of the day drumming up support for himself. So it took only one vote all around."

Instinctively Penny had the feeling Meecham might have been one of the men she had overheard. But there wasn't any point in repeating what she'd heard. It was too late. Meecham was in charge now.

Meecham, a tall unsmiling man with an arrogant stride and a harsh voice, went around the wagons after they were in their places for the night, barking orders and corrections to anything he could find to object to. Brad, like most of the Missourian men, would usually grumble in his wake. Although Brad didn't seem too happy about the selection either, he told Penny, "It's the same as on a ship at sea: the captain's word is law on the trail. You gotta hand it to him. He's keeping to the strict schedule of ten or fifteen miles a day. He's gettin' us to the mountains 'fore it snows."

Penny felt it best to keep her own comments to herself. Brad was right; maybe what they needed was a forceful, "no-nonsense" leader to get them to their destination safely.

Penny was keeping a lot of things to herself these days. Lately she had experienced an unexpected nostalgia for Dunwoodie. It would hit her at odd moments, mostly in the evenings at the end of a long day. Maybe it was the smell of wood fires or the plink of a guitar being picked hesitantly, its player trying for the right chord, or the sweet, sad twang of a harmonica, that would bring on a kind of homesickness. As a feeling of sadness came over her she would get busy at some chore, distracting herself. This homesickness didn't happen often. Most of the time, Penny realized she was having a "once-in-a-lifetime" experience and relished it.

The week of July Fourth, she wrote in Grams' letter-journal:

We reached Independence Rock, which seems a fitting place to celebrate the nation's birthday. We spent two days here, camping, doing our wash, and catching up on chores you can't get to when traveling. Some of the more adventurous among the younger men climbed up onto the rock to carve their names thereon — "for posterity," I suppose. Throughout our whole wagon train there's a certain feeling of pride that we've come this far. Many of us are as surprised as pleased that we've proved ourselves to be so hearty and have become seasoned campers, learning new skills. Of course, some of our fellow travelers have suffered greatly due to losses of children or spouses through illness or accident. But as you would say, Grams, it's all part of God's plan, and we'll know why someday.

Penny stopped here, wondering if she should mention that though they had been warned of the possible Indian raids, so far there had been no sign of any hostile Indians. A few mildly annoying ones followed them as they drew nearer to Fort Laramie, begging and wanting to barter, but they soon disappeared. Better pickin's farther from the fort, everyone guessed. Deciding not to mention the Indians, Penny went back to writing.

The celebration started early in the day by the most verbal and visible "patriots." There was speechifying, pounding on tin pots and pans, rifles and pistol shots into the air, yells and wild whooping, hollering and shouts. The men gathered in small groups to talk politics loudly. Sometimes these "discussions" became shouting, while tempers and patriotism ran high and got mixed-up. A few even ended in fisticuffs. Although there is a rule about no whiskey or other spirits on the train, somebody had smuggled in something that was at the root of most of the disturbances.

Late in the afternoon all we ladies put on our "best bib and tucker," as Nelldean calls it, and everyone joined in for a barbecue and some high jinks for the children. In the evening guitar and banjo, with accompaniment of several mouth organs, provided music for some square dancing. The children were allowed to run wild while the grown-ups enjoyed the release from the deadening drudgery of trail life. The party went far into the night, and everyone declared it a high mark of the long journey.

Neither Jeremiah nor Emily put in an appearance at the Fourth of July celebration. It was the kind of gathering that Jeremiah probably considered "unseemly" — well, maybe it was for someone as inflexible as Jeremiah. But it was certainly the kind of harmless relaxation that most of the weary travelers needed. Penny's sympathy for Jeremiah's unfortunate wife mounted.

Chapter 12

FORT LARAMIE

The night before they reached the military post at Fort Laramie, the guides, as usual, rode back down the line of wagons telling each driver where they would camp overnight. Penny, who was riding Mariah alongside the wagon, heard the scout shout up to Brad, "Twenty miles today — good day's trek. We're pulling out about a mile from the fort and camping there."

Fort Laramie would be the first chance in all the long weeks of travel to replenish supplies and stock up on some things like salt and sugar, which were running low.

The very next morning the fort's commander, with two aides, rode out to welcome the wagon train. He was an impressive-looking man, with a narrow, handsome face and a full mustache, the epitome of a West Point graduate, all "spit and polish." The wagon master and the Iowan captain, Thomas Meecham, met him. Through them the colonel issued an invitation to the emigrants to attend the dress parade of his soldiers that afternoon.

Eagerly Penny and Thea looked forward to this rare diversion from the monotony of life on the trail. They put on their sunbonnets and, carrying Belinda, found a shady spot from which to watch the cavalry officers go through their paces. The uniformed men, erect in their saddles, the sun gleaming on their swords belted to their gilt sashes, presented a splendid sight. At the different bugle calls, their mounts were instantly alert, their ears twitching, the arched necks taut. Then on signal the beautiful animals, in perfect alignment, wheeled and marched in formation, with never a misstep nor a wrong turn. It was thrilling, and Penny felt a sense of pride simply watching the riders in well-trained troops go through their paces. They could not have done better if they were being reviewed by the president as commander-in-chief of the army himself.

To their further excitement and surprise, later that afternoon officers from the fort arrived at the camp to invite all the ladies to a dance to be held that evening at the headquarters.

"Oh, of course, you must go, Penny," Thea said. "It will be good for you to get dressed up for a change, do some dancing and a little flirting!"

"I don't want to go by myself!" protested Penny. "They invited *all* the ladies, you know. *You* can go too."

Thea's cheeks flushed, a glint of possibility showing in her eyes. She ventured hesitantly, "Do you think Brad would? . . ."

"Let's ask him," suggested Penny, adding with a teasing smile, "He can't object if we take Belinda along for a chaperone!"

They laughed merrily at the thought and went together to look for Brad. They found him talking to Mr. Walker, who looked amused when the two girls posed the question. Brad hesitated only a minute, glancing over at the older man, who gave an imperceptible nod. Then Brad smiled. "Don't see why not. You two deserve a little fun. Just so long as you keep your wedding ring and Belinda in plain sight, Thea," he cautioned with mock severity.

Back at the wagon Thea opened her small humpbacked trunk and began digging into its depths. "Here, Penny," she said, holding out her lace shawl. "You must wear this and carry my fan."

The rest of the afternoon the girls pondered what to wear, primped, and practiced new hairstyles in a frenzy that reminded them of old times. They giggled until they were quite giddy.

"Here, try this." Thea tossed Penny her lace shawl to add an elegant touch to the simply made, periwinkle-blue dress. Thea's early pregnancy had just given her tiny figure a pleasant roundness. They hid the fact that the last hooks on her bodice didn't meet by cleverly adding a wide sash to her full-skirted, peppermint pink-striped dress. At last they were ready. They got Belinda up from her nap, dressed her in her prettiest dress and ruffled bonnet, then went to show Brad before leaving.

"Never saw three prettier young ladies," he told them.

"Sure you don't want to come along?" Thea asked.

"And spoil the soldiers' evening?" he teased. "Nah! You all go along and have a good time."

They left him at the wagon and went to join the contingent of other wagon train ladies waiting for the promised transportation over to the fort.

There was a flurry of exchanged compliments as the women eyed each other's hurriedly assembled finery. A good number of ladies had shown up for the night's festivities, even some of the older ones, like Nelldean. They had no intention of dancing, but just were hungry for some music, some gaiety, and some lighthearted fun. Penny noted that Emily Bradshaw was not in the group. Probably Jeremiah had not allowed her to come. Poor soul! If anyone needed a little change, it was someone confined to the company of the dour Jeremiah all these weeks.

Soon the wagon sent by the fort's commander arrived. With much laughter and joking the ladies were helped up into it by courteous soldiers. As they set off toward the fort they had an escort of four cavalry men in spotless blue uniforms, brass buttons blazing, boots shining. They were mounted on gleaming horses and rode alongside.

As they mounted the wooden steps into a mess hall, which had been transformed for the occasion, Penny could hear music. All at once, all her worries and doubts of the last few weeks that had been so hard to shake fell away like magic.

Later Penny described the evening to Grams:

The minute we stepped inside we were surrounded — ambushed might be the "military" way to say it — by officers, all of whom were handsome, charming, and gracious — and clamoring for a dance. Believe it or not, I was whirled away at once by a blonde, mustachioed man (a lieutenant, no less!), leaving a number of other disappointed young men looking soulful. (A totally *new* experience for me, especially attending a dancing party with *Thea!*)

But, as I'm told, at Fort Laramie, as in all army posts, especially one as isolated as this, the men always outnumber the available ladies. Only the senior officers are allowed to have their wives with them at this fort. The result of this rule is that for months many of these gentlemen have not set eyes on a woman, other than the wives of their superior officers or the Indian squaws who come in to trade. With so many bachelor officers doing their first duty after graduating from West Point, these were especially anxious to make the most of this rare social occasion. Having never known such popularity in Dunwoodie, I can tell you I was pretty nigh overcome. But Grams, I do have enough common sense to know that I couldn't possibly be as pretty, as witty, or as good a dancer as I was told over and over during the evening. I am also human enough to thoroughly enjoy such attention.

Not that Thea was left on the sidelines, by any manner of means. As usual, her picture-perfect beauty, her sweet smile, and her manners had her at the center of male admiration. The few times I had a chance to glance her way, she was always at the center of an admiring coterie of officers. Sometimes engaged in conversation with one or more officers while Belinda was held alternately by one or the other. That young lady — probably a foretaste of things to come, when *she* will certainly be the "belle of the ball" — was having the time of her young life, clapping her tiny hands happily to the tunes of the regiment's band who were providing the dance music. Nelldean took over the lap-sitting several times during the evening so Thea could dance. I saw her gracefully waltzing with one or the other of her attentive officer admirers. It was so good to see her happy and not anxious as she has sometimes been on this journey.

A buffet supper was served at midnight — food such as our sore eyes have not beheld in many a long day! Platters of sliced ham, turkey, salads, spiced peaches, bowls of nuts, relishes, and a raspberry "bombe." Such an astonishing array was set forth that I was hard put not to "make a spectacle of myself," as you would say, Grams. After weeks of the monotonous trail diet I had to exert great control not to try everything and seconds at that!

After that there was more dancing. Finally, to accumulated groans of protest from the gentlemen, the band struck up the traditional "Good Night, Ladies," and the unusual evening came to an end.

We ladies were reluctantly led back to the wagon in which we'd arrived and again escorted back to the wagon camp, this time accompanied by more than a dozen officers who had saddled up to escort us home in style.

When Penny finished this description of the party at Fort Laramie, she tore it out of the notebook and folded it in with the other journal-letters she'd written, planning to mail them at the post exchange when they went there the following day to replenish their supplies.

The next day, Penny and Thea wanted to take advantage of the chance to stock up. While Brad worked on the wagon, oiling the axle, checking wheels, renailing the sideboards that had loosened on the miles of jolting travel, Nelldean accompanied Penny and Thea, carrying Belinda, to buy provisions at the fort's store.

It was good to see all that was stocked there. Although only a few wives of army officers were posted so far west with their husbands, the store had many things that would catch the feminine eye: bolts of brightly colored materials, ribbons and bonnet trims, buttons, and yards of lace and eyelet ruffles. Even though they could not afford much, Thea and Penny enjoyed looking at all the luxuries, almost forgetting the list they had compiled. Penny was particularly tempted by a patterned paisley when she felt Thea pinch her arm and whisper, "Look over there."

"What?" Penny glanced questioningly at her sister-in-law. Thea shifted her eyes slightly to the right. Penny looked in the direction Thea indicated. All she saw was a tall, slender, dark-haired young woman standing nearby. Penny gave a shrug and glanced back, puzzled, at Thea. Just then the woman turned her head toward Penny, and she realized why Thea wanted her to see the young woman. Though otherwise attractive, the young woman's face was oddly disfigured with black markings. Her clear, gray eyes met Penny's stare coldly; then deliberately she turned her attention back to the length of red calico she had been examining. Embarrassed, Penny quickly began to discuss with Thea the idea of making new sunbonnets for the three of them.

A few minutes later the strangely marked young woman made her purchase, then left the store. Penny hoped that she hadn't made her feel self-conscious. She almost felt like going after her to apologize. But that would only make matters worse. Surely she must be used to people's curious glances.

"What do you suppose happened to *her?*" Thea asked.

Nelldean came up alongside them. "You're curious about the girl who was just in here?"

"We didn't mean to be rude."

"No, of course you didn't. I saw her the other day and asked one of the soldier's wives about her. It's a sad story actually. Her name is Celina Preston. She's the foster daughter of some people here at the fort. But when she was not much older than Belinda, her whole family was attacked by some marauding Apaches. All the rest of the family were killed except her and her sister. They were both taken captive. No one knows for sure what happened to the sister, but about four years later Celina was found. She'd been traded to the Mojave Indians by the Apaches, and that is their custom. They cut into the flesh, then rub charcoal or dye into the wounds." Nelldean shook her head. "She was brought to the fort and adopted by some people who had known her real family. They've tried to erase those tattoo marks but — it's not easy, no easier than erasing the memories of her years with the savages."

Thea, visibly moved by the story, shuddered and clutched Belinda closer.

"Does that happen often?" she asked. "Indians taking children?"

"Not often, although it does happen —" Then, sensing Thea's unspoken fear, Nelldean spoke reassuringly, "But the Indians around here and from this point on are mostly friendly. I haven't heard of a wagon train being attacked for a long time."

All Penny's recollections of Fort Laramie would have been pleasant ones if it had not been for one horrifying incident just before the wagon train pulled out to continue its westward journey.

One morning she, Thea, and Nelldean went to do some last-minute shopping at the fort's commissary. They were just leaving the store to walk back to their wagon when the sound of screaming reached their startled ears. It was so frighteningly high-pitched, like a wounded animal or some tortured creature, that they stopped dead in their tracks, clutching each other in fear. As they stood on the commissary porch, an army ambulance came rattling around the corner of the building. The two horses pulling it scrambled to keep their footing as the vehicle careened almost on two wheels. At the front of the infirmary on the quadrangle of the officers' quarters, the driver shouted a loud "Whoa!" and pulled the horses to a skittering halt.

As Penny and Thea stared, the soldier beside the driver jumped down from the seat and ran back to the ambulance's double doors. A minute later, two uniformed men emerged from the infirmary dragging a woman between them. Her hair was wild and streaming behind her, she was tightly held by both arms but struggling, kicking and yelling for them to let her go. Following them out onto the porch were two uniformed men. One, his head bowed, obviously distraught, was supported by a fellow officer as he walked unsteadily from the door of the building. He was openly weeping as the men holding the still-screaming woman finally lifted her into the ambulance and climbed in after her. The doors were slammed shut and bolted, and they all drove off. In silent horror, Penny and Thea watched, their eyes widened in shock.

Nelldean, who had followed them out of the store came alongside, saying in a sad tone of voice, "Poor woman! The storekeeper told me she's one of the officer's wives. They're taking her back east. Hopefully, once she's back in familiar surroundings, and with her family if she's got one, she'll recover." Nelldean shook her head. "Some people can't take it. It's especially hard on women, left alone much of the time when their soldier husbands are gone for weeks or even months on patrol. Go mad with the isolation, the loneliness. Tragic for her husband as well. . . ."

Some movement behind her caught Penny's attention. She half turned just in time to see Emily Bradshaw standing a short distance away in the entrance to the fort commissary. Penny had not noticed her in the store, but she too must have witnessed the dreadfully distressing scene. As Penny turned, Emily dropped her shopping basket and swayed, then clung to the wooden frame, her face ashen. She looked as if she might faint.

Spontaneously Penny went over to her. "Are you all right?" she asked. "Maybe you should sit down. I'll see if I can get you some water."

Just then a man's voice spoke harshly, "We don't need your help."

Penny recognized that voice and whirled around to see Jeremiah striding toward them. He brushed rudely by her. "I can take care of my wife. We can manage."

Immediately Penny stepped back. Jeremiah took his wife's arm, keeping her from sagging to the ground. "Come, Emily." She leaned against him as if all her strength had left her. He roughly grabbed her basket, then, still holding her by her arm, half dragged her down the steps and across the compound in the direction of the wagon train.

Biting her lip in helpless indignation, Penny's hands clenched. How insensitive Jeremiah was! Couldn't he have shown his wife some compassion, some gentleness?

Nelldean echoed her thoughts. "I'm afraid that poor, poor woman is one of those I meant. I doubt if she'll make it, one way or another." Thea looked pale and shocked. Linking arms, they walked back to their wagons. Both scenes had brought sharply into focus the dangers, the risks, the terrible possibilities of what they had never realized at the outset of the journey west.

In the days that followed these two heart-rending scenes flashed vividly into Penny's mind. She kept seeing the girl with the tattooed face and the mad woman. Although they never discussed it, Penny was sure Thea was haunted by them too. Penny wondered at Nelldean's seeming acceptance of the horrors that sometimes happened in the western territories. But then she must have seen it often:

the hopelessness of women broken by their husband's choices and expressing it in various ways — some by accepting it and saying, "nothing to do but stay"; others by plunging into madness.

One day when she and Nelldean were walking together, Penny confided, "I can't get that officer's wife out of my head. It makes me wonder about myself, if I would crack like that given her circumstances."

Nelldean shook her head emphatically. "Not you, Penny. *You've* got the stuff. I spotted that in you right away. And I've watched you. You ain't afraid to take on somethin' you've never tried before," she chuckled. "You've got what they call the 'pioneer spirit' and a bit of stubbornness too, I reckon. No siree, Penny, I'd count on *you* makin' it no matter what."

Nelldean's appraisal comforted Penny a little. Still she hoped she would never be put to the test.

Chapter 13

Penny was concerned about Thea. Brad was too busy with all his responsibilities to notice, but as the days went on, Penny was very conscious of Thea's waning strength. The ceaseless rattling of the wagon gave her headaches, and sometimes she seemed so lethargic, sometimes so dazed with fatigue, that she did not seem to notice what was going on. More and more, Penny took over the care of Belinda who, at two and a half, was becoming quite a handful. She was so active now and into everything. She had to be watched every waking minute to keep her out of mischief and away from disaster. They had to be careful not to set thoughtlessly aside a knife or a boiling pot unattended. Her curiosity was unlimited. One day she nearly fell head first into a bucket of drinking water. Another time she picked up a greasy discarded rag Penny had used to scour a skillet and stuffed it happily into her mouth. It was all Penny could do to keep up with her. As for Thea, all her efforts seemed to be in garnering her energy to put on an animation and cheerfulness she could not really feel when Brad was around.

Penny would place Belinda in front of her in the saddle when she rode Mariah so that Thea could rest in the back of the wagon. Penny's thoughts were often troubled. Thea should probably have never have come. In a way, Penny blamed herself. Maybe *she* had been wrong not to tell Grams about Thea's condition and seek her advice as to whether Thea should attempt the journey. A word from Grams would have been enough to cause Brad to postpone their leaving at least until after the baby arrived. But it was too late now. She would just have to pray that they would reach California in good health and everything would be all right.

After leaving Fort Laramie, thinking they had said good-bye to "civilization" until they reached California, Penny and Thea mentally prepared themselves for the miles of wilderness stretching before them. To their amazement, the wagon train encountered eastbound visitors almost daily — travelers, some of whom had already made the western trek several times. The wagon train people surrounded them, eager to hear the confirmation of their hopes and dreams. Although the more skeptical among them doubted some of the "tall tales," for most it served to spur some of their original enthusiasm to see the country to which they themselves were headed.

The plains seemed to go on endlessly, broken here and there by jutting boulders or a mammoth rock structure. Heat shimmered relentlessly from the sun, turning the endless prairie into a tawny ochre. Before them they could see razor-edged buttes rising sharply and thrusting into the cloud-studded sky.

As they got closer to those jutting rocks what still lay ahead of the weary travelers began to dawn on them. The ever-present urgency to get through the Sierra before the chance of an early snow was always lurking in their minds. Now the morning and late-evening air had an autumn chill to it. All the livestock began to act strange, restless, spooky. Penny noticed it and mentioned it to Brad, who told her someone said it was the altitude that sometimes made them a little crazy.

That night, a men's meeting was called, and afterward, when Brad returned and joined Thea and Penny at the campfire where they sat waiting for him, his expression had a firm set.

"We've got to ditch some of our stuff. There's no other way. Everybody's going to have to do it. The wagons are overloaded, the oxen and mules' strength dangerously strained . . . now, you both look over your things . . . from now on we only take necessities. Everything else's got to go . . . no exceptions."

Knowing her softhearted, easygoing brother, Penny realized he was putting on as stern a face as possible. From her own experience she knew Brad could be wheedled. Certainly Thea, in her gentle way, could most often win any argument. But this was different. Word had gone out from the captain that if they wanted to avoid disaster and make California before a blizzard trapped them in one of the mountain passes, the teams' loads had to be lightened.

They all retired in a somber mood. Brad's last words were, "Tomorrow morning we got to pile all the things we're not taking on the side of the road. So be thinking about it tonight. And by the way, ladies, I have the last word."

Penny might have smiled at her brother's warning. He was girding himself beforehand from any pleading, forlorn sighs, or wistful tears on their part.

Penny slept in the tent that night beside Belinda, leaving the wagon for Brad and Thea by themselves, thinking they might need some privacy to discuss the matter. When she woke up at daylight the next morning, she heard the low murmur of their voices and from the tone, she realized things had not been settled.

"No, Thea, I told you not to bring it in the first place. It's got to go along with the barrel of china and the clock . . . I'm sorry, but they're just too heavy. I can't make it any clearer — we've got orders."

Penny had never heard her brother speak so abruptly to his wife.

"Now, don't argue, Thea. And don't you dare cry! That's all there is to it."

Penny peeked out the flap of her tent and saw Brad jump down from the back of the wagon and stride off. Thea flung a shawl over her shoulders and ran to catch up with him.

Penny felt sure it was the cradle they were arguing about. Now Thea would *have* to tell him about the baby. And high time too! It's a wonder he hadn't noticed something. Thea's slender figure had daily rounded. But Brad was too distracted, too occupied with the demands of the relentless onward push during the day. At night he was so exhausted he nodded over his supper and soon flung himself into the wagon to sleep until dawn.

Penny left Belinda still curled up in her quilt, thumb in mouth, soundly asleep, and crept outside. She got the fire started, sliced some strips of bacon, and got out the last of the eggs to fry.

Within fifteen minutes she saw them walking slowly back to the campsite, Brad's arm around Thea's waist, her head resting on his shoulder. Brad looked dazed; Thea was smiling complacently.

When they stacked the extra trunk filled with embroidered linens, the bird's-eye maple chest of drawers, the china barrel, the Seth Thomas clock alongside some of the other emigrants' belongings and family heirlooms, the spool cherry cradle was not among them.

Penny was relieved that Brad had been told about the expected baby. It took some of the responsibility off her shoulders. She had disliked being a party to deception. She gave Brad credit that he never admonished her about it, never made a single reproving remark about her being a conspirator. He was simply a little more serious, showing Thea a little more consideration than usual. Penny knew he must be pleased at the possibility of having a son in the new land to where they were going.

In her letter-journal letter to Grams, Penny didn't have the heart to tell about all the things they had to leave behind on the road. It was hard enough to see how heartbroken Thea was. She had put on a brave face for

Brad, but when they were alone she had not been able to keep back the tears.

"Maybe it's because I never felt I had a real home when I was growing up. I so much wanted Belinda to have the few things from *my* mother when we built our new home in California," she sobbed. "You don't know how much those things meant to me."

"Yes, I do understand." Penny tried to comfort her. "But Belinda will have other things, Thea. New kinds of things. In California everything will be different. She won't even miss those things, because she won't know anything about them."

As they traveled further, Penny and Thea saw that the members of their wagon train group weren't the only ones who'd had to discard belongings to make the burden on the mules and oxen lighter. Strewn all along the rutted trail were quilts, chests, trunks, rocking chairs, clocks, and sets of dishes. All sad reminders of cherished items some woman had shed tears over leaving behind. But even among themselves the women did not complain. They had come this far and were beginning to realize how far they had yet to go. The men's weary eyes told the story more clearly than anything they could say.

Chapter 14

A few days after the "great ditching," as Penny and Thea called the wistful discarding of special belongings, when the wagon train stopped at noon to feed and rest the animals, they decided to rearrange the interior of the wagon. With the addition of the new supplies purchased at Fort Laramie, even after the elimination of items Brad deemed "unnecessary," the inside of the wagon still seemed crowded. Working hard and fast, they soon became hot and tired. The canvas interior was cramped and stuffy. Finally Thea brushed back her hair from her damp forehead with the back of her arm, saying, "Whew, I've got to stop for a few minutes."

One glance at Thea's flushed face reminded Penny sharply of her sister-in-law's delicate condition, and she quickly agreed, "It's near noon anyway. Let's quit. Go outside and cool off. I'll go get us some water, and we'll make some lemonade." She held up the bottle of citrus oil they'd bought at the post store on Nelldean's suggestion that it was a passable substitute for the fruit to make lemonade. Thea seemed relieved and leaned wearily against the back of the wagon while Penny grabbed one of the pails and headed for the water barrel.

Brad was checking the wooden wheels, testing for cracks, tightening ropes, and generally looking over everything. Belinda played on the ground in the shade thrown by the arched top of the wagon.

It was hot. The sun beat down mercilessly as Penny came back lugging the heavy pail of water. They had a time discussing how much oil to pour into their cups before adding water, and then they sampled and tasted until the right mixture was achieved.

They offered a cup to Brad, who welcomed it, and Thea held one to Belinda's mouth for her to drink some, spilling most. Thea had pleated paper into fans, and they sat sipping their makeshift lemonade, chatting idly while enjoying the respite.

Suddenly a terrifying cry split the air and went ricocheting up and down the line of parked wagons: "Indians!"

At the screams of terror echoing from one wagon to the other both women looked at each other wide-eyed with fear. Thea seemed paralyzed with fright, while Penny was galvanized into action. She scrambled to her feet and snatched up Belinda. Reaching for

Thea's hand, she jerked her to her feet then pointed to the wagon. "Under the wagon. Hurry!"

Brad was running toward them, waving both hands and shouting for them to hurry and take shelter under the wagon as Penny had said. Then he grabbed his shotgun. Penny shoved Thea first, then, clutching Belinda, Penny crawled after Thea. They lay there trembling with Belinda between them.

Dust whirled like great windmills from the thundering hooves of what seemed like hundreds of horses galloping past. The air was splintered with the sound of frenzied whoops and screeching yells. The sun glinted on the red-bronze skin of bare-chested men with garishly painted faces as they thundered by the wagon where the women were hidden. Colorful headbands, bright feathers, long black braids, streamed behind as the Indians circled the wagons, brandishing spears and bows. Arrows whistled and popped with a sizzling sound as the riders turned their ponies sharply, causing them to skid as they swirled in a kind of wild dance. The pong and swish of bow strings and arrows mingled with the snapping crack of rifles as the wagon train men tried to scare the Indians off.

Terrified, shuddering at each shot, Penny and Thea squeezed each other's hands in a painful grip. Was this the kind of attack others had related in detail? Would the horrors of scalping, capture, torture, and worse follow? Eyes widened with shock, they stared at each other, speechless but questioning. Penny squinted into the sun's glare, trying to see what was happening. But dust clouds obscured her view. Then Thea began sobbing and Belinda started to cry. Penny put her arm over Thea's shaking shoulders and huddled closer, her own heart hammering out of control. Then just as suddenly as they had appeared, the Indians whirled around and, still yelling at the top of their lungs, galloped back up over the hill from where they had come. An eerie silence hung over the wagon train for at least a minute or two. Then suddenly, it was broken by great cries of relief rising up throughout the camp.

It wasn't until later that they discovered that, while part of the band had distracted the men of the wagon train by circling, shooting arrows, and yelling, other Indians had ridden over to where the horses were grazing and made off with some. To Penny's horror, Mariah had been taken.

Counting the losses, the men stood shaking their heads, trying to figure out how to divide the remaining ones and how to shift the weights in some of the wagons.

Sorrowfully Penny went back to their wagon. She wept unrestrained tears. The theft of her beloved mare, who had gallantly come this far with her, was a bitter loss.

The whole wagon train was sobered by the Indian raid. Although they were thankful no lives had been lost, the episode left everyone badly shaken.

There was no more grousing from the men about taking guard duty. Nerves were on edge. Trigger-sharp tempers flared over trivial things. Children got slapped by anxious mothers, who tried to keep them close by telling them dread tales of Indians taking little ones as hostage. Even the animals, sensing the humans' nervousness, were restless and spooked at the slightest sound.

In the evenings when people gathered around campfires, voices were low and tense. That was why everyone jumped one night when a woman's screams rent the air. Men reached for their rifles, and general confusion erupted. The screams soon dwindled to heartrending sobs. Startled people asked one another: Where were they coming from? Who was it? The silence that followed was almost eerie. Then the rumor ran through the wagon train like a prairie bush fire. The screams had come from the Bradshaw wagon. Emily

Bradshaw was in hysterics. Nelldean and one of the other older women hurried over to see if they could help. The quiet that descended on the whole train was ominous. One by one each family went into their wagons, pulled the canvas curtains and kept whatever they were thinking to themselves.

Penny, however, waited outside her own small tent until she saw Nelldean making her way back to her wagon and stopped her.

"We gave her a dose of laudanum; that should calm her down and help her sleep. Her husband was beside himself." Nelldean shook her head. "More angry than worried, I'd say. A strange man. . . ."

"He is, very strange indeed," Penny said, then in a burst of confidence she poured out her own experience with Jeremiah.

The older woman looked concerned. "I've seen his kind afore. So sure of themselves that it don't matter about other folks. He's right and you're wrong. Sad to say, a lot of the Lord's business is spoiled by the likes of him. . . ." She patted Penny's arm. "Just be thankful you didn't listen to him, and you're not in that poor girl's place."

With that Nelldean went on to her own wagon, leaving Penny to her troubled thoughts. She wished she could do something to help Emily Bradshaw. But she knew it would only be rejected and probably misinterpreted. It was a long time before she could fall asleep.

Penny was now regularly getting up and starting the breakfast, giving Thea the chance to rest in the wagon until Belinda woke up. One morning, two days after Emily Bradshaw's outburst, Penny went to get the water before the rest of the family awakened. Suddenly, as she was drawing water, she heard a man's voice behind her. "Penny, I have to talk to you."

Knowing at once who it was, she stiffened. She dreaded another ugly scene but did not know how to avoid it. For a long moment all was silent, except for the trickle of the water from the barrel into the pail. Still holding her pail under the spigot, she slowly turned to face Jeremiah.

His face was set in grim lines. There were circles under his heavy-lidded, bloodshot eyes, evidence of sleeplessness. His voice was strangely lifeless as he said, "I just wanted you to know we're turning back."

"You're turning back?" she repeated in surprise, then turned off the spigot.

"Yes. Emily isn't well . . . not well at all. I've talked to Captain Harding. He tells me that there should be an army patrol coming by here soon on their way back to the fort. We could travel with them as an escort in case —," he halted as if it were difficult to continue, "— of Indians again. You see, it's the fear — she can't take anymore . . . her nerves, her physical strength. . . . I'll have to take her home. Some others are also leaving the wagon train. There'll be enough to be safe. . . ."

The note of defeat in his voice was strong. In spite of all that had passed between them, Penny could not help feeling sorry for him. Going west and being a missionary was what had driven him with such intensity. Wrongheaded as he might have been about *her,* this was still something he had deeply wanted for himself and for the woman he had married. To give up now seemed tragic. One look at his stricken expression revealed what a crushing blow this decision had been for him. How was she to express her sympathy without sounding false?

"I'm sorry, Jeremiah . . . I know how much coming west meant to you. . . . This must be a terrible disappointment. But of course, you must do what you need to do for Emily's sake —"

Jeremiah harshly cut her short. "It's *your* fault, you know."

"*My* fault?" The accusation stunned her. "How could it be *my* fault?"

His voice roughened angrily, "If *you* had not been rebellious and done what you were supposed to have done . . . this wouldn't have happened. If you had *listened* and *obeyed as you were supposed to do!* It would have been you and I, together. *You're* strong, Penny. *Physically* strong but weak morally." His mouth twisted in a sneer. "If *you* had only obeyed —"

Penny held up a warning hand, "Stop, Jeremiah! I don't want to hear this, and I won't listen —"

He reached out and gripped her upper arm. "But you will hear it, and you will listen. *Now* you *will* listen. Before you refused to, but see what your willfulness has brought about? *Your* pride has brought about destruction, just as I knew it would." His voice became louder, ragged with emotion. "It was the Lord's will for *us* . . . *you* and me, not Emily —"

"No, Jeremiah! Don't say another word. It's wrong —" She lowered her voice, but she stared at him steadily. "Have you ever thought you might have mistaken the message? It's *you* who could be wrong, Jeremiah."

He shook his head, his voice cracked as he gripped her arm. "Penny, I loved you — *we* could have made it."

"No, Jeremiah . . . no." Determinedly she pried his fingers from her arm. "Don't say anything more you'll be sorry for. We shouldn't be having this conversation. Please go. Emily is your wife. She needs you. This must be difficult for her knowing she is disappointing you and yet — she cannot go on. You should be with her . . . just go."

The muscle in his cheek quivered as he struggled to regain his composure. His eyes were like burning coals. His mouth worked as if he still wanted to say something more. Gradually he loosened his hold and dropped her arm. Then just as suddenly as he had come, he turned and walked slowly away, his shoulders hunched, a broken man, his dream of glory shattered.

Had Emily's breakdown been brought on by witnessing the woman who had to be trussed and dragged into the ambulance a short time before? Had Emily been afraid of what might be awaiting her in some isolated mission post? Or was she having nightmares of what still might lie ahead along the endless trail before them, before they even got to California? Had the mere idea of it weakened her resolve and broken her spirit?

In the camps there were rumors, especially among the women, who spoke in low voices, afraid of being overheard. They told tales of relatives or friends of theirs who had been broken by the experience of the trail. The oftenheard phrase "Nothing to do but stay" came to Penny's mind. They were at the half-way mark. A few days more and they would reach the "No Return Trail" — after which there would be no turning back.

Early one morning a few days later, Penny heard the sounds of horses' hooves and wagon wheels. She looked out through the flap of her tent to see Jeremiah's wagon and two others departing, escorted by a patrol of blue-uniformed troopers. Two other families had also decided it was too risky to go on. Watching them go, Penny was conscious of a funny sensation in the pit of her stomach. She knew one of the women who was leaving was expecting a child about the same time as Thea, and much as she tried not to let it, that worried Penny.

Penny shivered involuntarily. Had *they* made a terrible mistake to come? After the halfway point, it would be longer and more dangerous for anyone to turn around, one wagon alone along all those dreary, desolated miles. Penny pushed away all those daunting thoughts. Of course Brad would never turn back. Besides, things were going to work out beautifully for *them*. They would find a wonderful homestead, their crops would flourish just like people said, Belinda would be healthy and happy, and Thea would have the new baby, born in California, a son for Brad.

Ahead lay the Snake River and the last leg of the long journey. There was an urgency now to get on the other side of the river, as far away as they could get from hostile Indian territory. Who knew for sure if the savages might not again swoop down from behind the hillsides any moment?

"It could have been worse," Brad said grimly, his eyes traveling to his wife and child. Penny knew the fears that must be lurking in his mind. She tried to echo his comment, although her heart was still sore from the loss of Mariah. She now walked, carrying Belinda most of the time — to ease the burden of their oxen. Now that Brad knew about the coming baby, Penny felt some of the weight of guilt lifted. She didn't like keeping secrets. Also, Thea now did not try to hide her discomfort, her general ill health. Pathetic in her apologies, she more and more let Penny take the responsibility for Belinda.

Brad too relied more and more on Penny's help. He didn't want to ask anything of Thea that might be beyond her strength. So he started teaching Penny how to drive the wagon. He'd get her to take the reins once or twice a day. At first she found it totally different from riding a saddle horse or driving a light buggy with one horse. Her shoulder muscles ached with the strain, and her hands became a mass of blisters. But she had always had a stubborn, competitive spirit and now wanted to prove to her brother that she was equal to the challenge.

Chapter 15

The Snake River

As they camped the night before they were to cross the Snake River a circuit of unspoken apprehension vibrated throughout the wagon train. There was a sense that danger lay ahead. The uncertainty of the undertaking made the worried men tense and apt to argue. Once more, tempers flared and brief arguments erupted into fights. That evening it clouded up ominously. Rain the next day would make visibility worse and make a safe crossing doubly difficult. A chill wind blew, which set the horses whinnying, the mules braying, and the heavy oxen moving uneasily.

During the night it rained lightly. Penny heard the patter on the canvas overhead. She heard Brad moving restlessly on the other side of the wagon and knew he was sleepless with worry about the next day's ordeal.

At Penny's first sight of the river, she realized why Brad had been so vigilant in training her to handle the wagon, adamant that she become competent. It was a scary prospect. Brad busied himself checking the ropes on the canvas, nailing any loose boards on the body of the wagon. Tersely he ordered Thea to take Belinda into the wagon, to secure themselves in a nest of quilts wedged in between the storage chests, and not to move until they got to the other side of the river.

As each wagon moved up to the bank in turn, Penny grew more nervous. She was sitting on the driver's seat beside Brad. Every so often she glanced over and saw his jaw was clenched, his eyes straight ahead, almost holding his breath as he watched wagon after wagon being pulled into the rushing river by the frightened animals. The wagon train had crossed other rivers on their way west, but none as wide as this one. There was only one wagon ahead of them now. It started down the bank, while its driver held tightly onto his mules' harness and shouted. The wagon swayed heavily as it reached the water. Penny caught her breath, sure that it was going to tip over. Her attention was brought sharply to their own problem.

"Here, take these." Brad thrust the reins at her and she grabbed them. "I'm going to lead the oxen down. No matter what happens, hold on. We gotta get across."

Penny doubled the leather reins around her

wrists and held them tightly. She fastened her gaze on the opposite bank, not daring to look down, though out of the corner of her eyes she could see the floating debris of other wagons. Packs of possessions that had not been securely fastened had burst loose and were sailing downstream among the rocks and broken tree branches. It was frightening. Among all the sights and sounds around her, she was suddenly aware of the crack of Brad's whip as he urged the reluctant oxen into the water's rushing current. Penny tightened her grip on the reins. She could hear the hair-raising shrieks of the animals and the curses and shouts of the men. The turmoil was enough to chill the blood of even the bravest.

Then the wagon lurched and pitched as it hit the water. From inside she heard Thea's stifled screams and knew she must be terrified at the rocking motion of the wagon as they slid down the bank, then were caught up in the current. Behind her she felt the canvas flap like sails as the wind ripped through it. Her heart felt as though it were in her throat. Every prayer she had ever learned flew to her mind until all she could do was gasp between her chattering teeth, "Mercy! Mercy! *Help!*"

Then just as suddenly, Penny knew they had made it when she heard Brad's voice ring out heartily, "Good girl, Penny! Good for you!"

He pulled the still-frightened animals into place on the opposite bank; then he ran to the back of the wagon to check on Thea and Belinda. Too weak to congratulate herself, Penny drew a long, shaky breath. She was slowly pulling herself together when Brad came alongside and said, "Take care of Thea and the baby. I'm going to see if I can help some of the others."

Penny climbed down from the driver's seat. As she started to walk she realized her legs were wobbling. She had to hold on to the side of the wagon for a minute or two to steady herself before she could go around to check on Thea and Belinda. Thea was pale as cheese and looked as though she might be sick. She handed Belinda over to Penny and started to say something when they heard a piercing scream from the river. They both stiffened.

"Something's happened!" Thea gasped.

"I'll go see." Penny slung Belinda on her hip and ran down to where a group was clustered on the bank. A woman was sobbing hysterically and some others were trying to comfort her. "It's my boy! He's going to drown!" she was crying over and over. A man's voice rose above the rest:

"Come on, fellas, we gotta help pull them out. Get a rope, someone!"

Penny moved in closer. "What's going on?" she asked a couple standing at the edge of the crowd.

"A child fell out when a wagon tipped over. He was caught in the current, swept downstream. A man dove in to save him, but the current shifted and now *he's* in trouble."

A deep shiver shuddered through Penny. *Brad!* Instinctively his name sprang into her mind. Brad was an excellent swimmer. Summer days had always found him in the deep pond behind Grams' house. It would be natural for him to leap in to save a child. With Belinda in her arms, Penny pushed through the crush of people to stand at the edge of the churning river so she could see better. The onlookers, who at first seemed mesmerized by the drama taking place in front of them, had turned into a cheering section for the would-be rescuers.

Penny's premonition had been correct. It *was* Brad floundering in the whirlpool of the river. As he spun and turned she could see a child's arms flailing. Over and over, Brad's head went under the water. Then he came up holding the boy's head above water, both gulping desperately. She felt as though a steel vise were gripping her throat. She wanted to scream but could make no sound. She tried to pray but no words came. Her arms tightened around Belinda, who squirmed and twisted, saying, "Too tight, Auntie!" Distractedly Penny loosened her hold on the little girl.

A rope had been slung around the trunk of a tree and knotted at the base. The other end was thrown like a lasso out into the water. People were yelling frantically now. The rope — their one hope of rescuing the pair — had sunk out of sight.

The current was too strong, too swift. Man and boy, captured in its grip, were caught in its fast-moving flow, too fast for anyone to help. Someone whipped out a machete, whacked at a low-hanging branch, and tried to throw it to Brad. As everyone watched, horrified, Brad's arm rose out of the churning water, his hand making a futile grab for the branch. But before he could reach it, he was swept into the whirling vortex. They had one last glimpse of him as he struggled frantically in the spray; then his head went down, one hand lifted desperately above the water, then that disappeared as well.

The voices of those on the riverbank rose in unified moan, then died away in gasps and sobs as everyone realized it was too late. Brad Sayres and the boy he had fought so gallantly to save were beyond help, beyond hope.

Stunned, an unbelieving Penny stood rooted to the spot. There was a stirring in the crowd behind her. Intuitively Penny turned to see Thea, with wide frightened eyes in a white face, coming through the parted crowd. "What is it, Penny? What's happened?"

Penny's lips trembled as she stammered out the words, "It's Brad, Thea. He's — he tried to save a little boy from drowning and he. . . ." She let Belinda slip out of her arms onto the muddy grass at her feet and held out her arms to her sister-in-law. "Oh, Thea, I'm so sorry. . . ."

Devastated, the hushed crowd fell back, casting furtive glances upon the two women locked in each other's arms. Thea's head sank limply on Penny's shoulder, her fragile body like a dead weight against her. A grief too profound for tears bound both women. Belinda, sitting at their feet, tugged at Penny's skirt. And for the first time in her short life she was not immediately lifted into her aunt's comforting embrace.

Nelldean arrived while Penny and Thea were still standing paralyzed with shock on the riverbank. Gently she led them back to the wagon and helped Penny urge Thea to lie down, suggested a soothing dose of laudanum for the grief-stricken woman. Then she took Belinda, fed her, rocked and sang to her. Finally mother and daughter were both asleep, and an exhausted Penny joined Nelldean at the back of the wagon. "What now, Nelldean?" she asked brokenly. "What in the world do we do now?"

The older woman reached for Penny's hand, held it quietly, and said, "Anything Nate and I can do, honey, you know you can count on us."

"I know, Nelldean." Penny nodded. "But I don't know what we're going to do. Without Brad. I just don't know. It's too late to turn back, and Thea's condition . . . I just don't know how we can go on."

"First things first, Penny. One day at a time. That's how all of us get through the hard times in life. You're young and strong, and you'll make it."

"I wish I felt sure of that."

"Remember, Penny, the Lord gives us strength just for the day. That's all he promised. Lean on him. As the Scripture says, 'When I am weak, he is strong' and 'He will not fail thee, nor forsake thee.' That's been proven to me over and over in my life, Penny."

Penny nodded and squeezed Nelldean's hand, wishing somehow she could borrow her faith at this desolate moment when her own was lacking.

"And Nate and I will help in any way we can."

"Thank you, Nelldean, I'm grateful." Penny knew Nelldean meant what she said, but after all, she and Nate were going to Oregon, while Brad's homestead was in California. That's where *they* were headed. Or were they?

The next day, some of the men searching along the riverbank found the bodies of both Brad and the little boy he'd tried so hard to save. The urgency of "moving on" was the deciding factor; they had to ready them immediately for burial the following day. The wagon train was delaying its departure so that this could be done with some respect and decency.

That morning, Penny rose before dawn. Dazed with shock, she dressed Belinda and fed her breakfast. Penny was wrapped in a kind of wordless grief, like being swathed in cotton wool, beyond tears, beyond feeling.

Thea, due to the dosage of laudanum Nelldean suggested, remained traumatized, unaccepting of the reality of Brad's death.

Together the two women walked to the place of the improvised burial service. The parents of the little boy were in even worse emotional shape, the mother near collapse.

Penny kept her arm around Thea's waist, supporting her lest she faint. There was no minister with the wagon train, and a man she hardly knew read a passage from someone's Bible before lowering Brad's body into the shallow grave.

It still seemed so unreal that Brad, with all his boundless enthusiasm and optimism, was gone, that they would never see his teasing glance nor hear his laughter. He had been the spur for them all. Over and over he had told them they stood to gain everything by this journey. It never occurred to him that they would lose everything — his very life.

When the brief service was over they returned to the wagon where Nelldean had been keeping Belinda amused. With a meaningful glance at Penny she indicated another spoonful of laudanum might be in order for Thea.

"It will get her over this first part, at least. In a day or two there will be time enough for her to come to terms with it."

With some misgivings Penny did as Nelldean suggested. What good would a few hours of oblivion do when there was so much to decide? Was it all going to be up to *her?*

Nelldean took Belinda with her so Penny would have some time to herself and so the little girl could watch some of the older children run and play.

Left alone, Penny faced the questions that had to be confronted — even amidst the horror of the tragedy that had overtaken them. What would she and Thea and Belinda do now? They couldn't turn back, they'd come too far; and without an escort — two lone women and a child in a wagon alone? It was out of the question. But with no man to drive the wagon, mile after mile over the mountains they had yet to travel, and with all the dangers and hardships they might be facing — that too seemed out of the question.

She was no closer to a solution to their problem when late in the afternoon Nelldean brought Belinda back. Thea roused briefly to sip some tea, then closed her eyes wearily and went back to sleep. As soon as it got dark, worn out with sorrow and emotional strain, Penny lay down beside Belinda. It was a miserable night, getting increasingly cold. Penny cuddled Belinda close, and huddled, shivering and sleepless, half the night. Every so often she would awake with a start when she heard the horses spooking and snorting on the picket ropes.

The little girl's soft, gentle breathing soon assured Penny she had gone to sleep. It was then that all her own misery returned. The scene of Brad's drowning came back in all its horror. Her grief was compounded by bitterness. She felt a quick, hot anger at the betrayal — against the people who had enticed them on this fool's journey, so full of untold hardships, misery, unseen dangers — and with probably worse to come.

First things first, Nelldean had wisely counseled. There was no time to grieve, no time to waste. The rule of the wagon train was "A day lost is never regained." Out of respect for Brad and the little boy he had tried to rescue, the wagons remained at the river a full day. But tomorrow morning they would pull out. Penny knew the first thing she had to do was go to the wagon master and ask him if somehow they could go on to California without a "head of household." Perhaps some of the other men could take turns spelling her, driving their wagon. Brad had certainly helped others out many times.

Penny had never had much contact with the wagon master. Brad had made all their arrangements, and, of course, only the men met with him regularly when anything had to be decided or voted on. She knew she was taking a big chance going to him and asking this favor, but she had to try! What alternative did she have?

Early the next morning, leaving Belinda with Nelldean, Penny walked down the line of wagons to where she saw Captain Harding sitting on a stump. Straightening her spine, bracing her shoulders, even while her heart raced, she approached him. He was holding a tin of canned peaches, spearing one slice at a time out with the tip of his knife, then bringing it dripping to his mouth.

Penny cleared her throat. "Good morning, sir. I've come to discuss with you the possibility of our moving on with the wagon train. Now that my brother's . . . gone, my sister-in-law has claim to his homestead in California, and I see no other way than for us to continue on —"

The words faltered on her lips as Harding slowly turned his head toward her, his eyes narrowed. He wiped his mouth with the back of his hand before speaking.

"I'm sorrier than I can say about your brother, miss, but there's no way I can let two women and a baby — cain't take that kind of responsibility. In my train all the men pitch in to help out the others, take picket duty, help fix broken axles or wheels, take care of the livestock. A wagon with no man to share the work of the whole wagon train is a burden. I don't need any more problems, miss. The combined Missouri and Iowa parties give me 'nuf worries as it is," he drawled, shaking his head. "No, ma'am, we're still in Indian territory. Sure as God made little green apples there might be more trouble than we can handle. Best thing I can do is let you go with us far as Fort Hall, then you can wait there for an escort goin' back east."

He gave her a sour glance. He didn't add "where you belong," but he might as well have. Penny's indignation rose in spite of her despair. There seemed to be nothing more to say.

Fighting tears, Penny walked back to her wagon. Maybe if she had used these tears before — a woman's ploy — perhaps the wagon master would have softened. Maybe not. In a way, she could understand his point. Allowing them to continue might endanger all the people in the wagon train. He couldn't make an exception. Now it was up to her to figure out what the three of them were to do. To wait at Fort Hall for an escort back east seemed preposterous. They were more than halfway to California. To travel back through what they had already endured? And for what? To go back to Dunwoodie? And with Thea getting nearer and nearer to the birth of the baby? No, she had to think of something else. What, she had no idea.

Nelldean was waiting to hear the result of Penny's mission.

"He said no — out of the question." Penny lifted Belinda out of Nelldean's lap and cuddled her close. "He says we can go as far as Fort Hall, then stay there until we can get an escort back home. But Nelldean, how can I do that?"

"Well, honey, we'll just take it to the Lord. He'll show us what to do. Let's sleep on it, see what tomorrow brings."

Chapter 16

Nelldean left and Penny tried to settle for sleep. These last few nights, sleep had been hard to come by, not only because of worry but also the weather. It had been hot, almost windless. Afraid her tossing and turning might disturb Thea, who needed her rest, she decided to make a lean-to at the end of the wagon and sleep outside. She had taken a length of canvas and propped it up with staves. Hoping to soon fall asleep, Penny stretched out on her blanket roll and closed her eyes.

But sleep proved impossible. Too many unanswerable questions kept her from relaxing. Soon she was wider awake than ever. She tried to pray. Bits and pieces of Scripture came and went in and out of her mind. As a child on Saturday nights she would lie in bed going over and over the Bible verse that she was supposed to have memorized and would be required to recite the next day at Sunday school. Tonight she couldn't seem to recall even one verse completely.

He must *hear me,* she thought plaintively.

Nelldean believed *all* prayers were heard. But were they answered? Fragments floated just on the edge of her memory. But when she tried to capture them to repeat them for comfort, they faded away.

"Your word I have hidden in my heart." **Hidden, all right,** she thought ironically. *Why can't I remember something comforting, encouraging, strengthening? "If you abide in me and my words abide in you . . ." then what? "Thy Word," what is it, Lord? "A lamp unto my feet, a light unto my path —" That's what I need: a word of guidance. What shall I do, Lord? If I hide your Word in my heart, what then, Lord? "Then you will walk on your way safely, and your foot will not stumble. When you lie down, you will not be afraid. Yes, you will lie down, and your sleep will be sweet —"*

She felt herself slowly drifting off.

Then suddenly hands were shaking her, a desperate voice in her ear. "Penny, Penny, wake up!"

Startled, heart pounding, Penny woke up. Her eyes flew open. She pushed back her hair, rubbing her eyes. Thea was bending over her.

"What is it? What's the matter, Thea? What's wrong?"

"It's the baby."

"Belinda?" Penny struggled up into a sitting position. "Is she sick?"

"No, it isn't Belinda, it's *me*, Penny."

"*You?* But —" Her words were cut short even before she had formed her question. Thea's face suddenly contorted. She closed her eyes, drawing a long, agonizing breath. Her fingers dug into Penny's arm where she clutched it.

The stunning truth hit Penny. The *baby!* It was the *new* baby Thea was talking about. All this flashed through Penny's brain, which was now fully awake and aware. *This couldn't be happening. Not now! It is too soon. Weeks too soon! Thea isn't supposed to have the baby until we reach California!*

Penny reached out, eased Thea down onto her mat, and held her until the spasm passed. Slowly Thea let out a long breath. "I'm sorry, Penny," she whispered. "I thought it was just . . . I didn't wake you because I thought maybe . . . I hoped . . . but then, remembering how it was when Belinda was born . . . I'm pretty sure —"

Penny scrambled to her feet, grabbed her skirt, threw it over her head, twisted it around her waist and buttoned it, then reached for her blouse.

"I'll go get Nelldean," she gasped. "*She'll* know what to do."

"I hate being such a burden —," Thea said weakly.

"Don't talk nonsense. But if the baby's really coming, we'll need help," Penny said sharply, too afraid herself to be too sympathetic. "Here, I'll help you back into the wagon, then I'll run over to their wagon."

Penny put her arm around Thea, helped her get to her feet, then supported her as they made their halting way back to the wagon. Just as she was about to step up inside, another pain gripped Thea, and she grabbed Penny, moaning. Penny felt Thea shudder, and she tightened her hold. All the prayers she couldn't remember a few hours before came flooding back to her now.

"Oh, God, an ever present help in trouble. . . . Therefore we will not fear." She had never felt so afraid in her life. Penny gritted her teeth. Thea seemed to slump against her.

"Over?" Penny asked her.

"For now — but they're coming closer."

"Easy, easy," Penny cautioned as she helped Thea gently up into the wagon. She pushed a pillow under Thea's head, put another one at her back. Thea was shivering uncontrollably, and Penny put an extra quilt on top of her. "Now, don't worry. I'll be right back."

"Wait, Penny." Thea put out her hand, tugged her skirt.

"Why? What is it?" Penny asked, impatient at the delay. She was fighting panic. From the little she knew about childbirth, she knew there was a need for haste. At least *she* would feel better when someone older and more experienced was with her.

"You better take Belinda. Put her in your blanket roll —"

"Good idea," replied Penny, her breath coming fast. Quickly she lifted the peacefully sleeping child, who did not waken as she carried her out to the lean-to and gently put her down. Then she stuck her head back in the wagon. "You'll be all right until I get back with Nelldean?"

In the dim light from the cloud-shrouded moon, Thea's face was a pale mask; her eyes were closed, but she managed a slow nod and a murmur. Penny took it for a yes.

"I'll hurry, Thea, just hang on," she said breathlessly, and then she picked up her skirt and started running along the line of parked wagons to where Nate had parked the Hardisons'. Reaching it, Penny rushed along the side, bumping into Nelldean's tin dishpan hung there and sending it clattering. A dog barked at the noise, and Penny stumbled, then caught herself by grabbing the side of the wagon. A splinter from the rough wood jabbed sharply into her palm. Tears sprang into her eyes and she winked them back.

"Nelldean! Nelldean! Nate!" she called,

shaking the canvas flap on the back of their wagon. "Please, it's Penny!"

It seemed an eternity until she saw Nelldean's sleep-wrinkled face under a ruffled nightcab stick itself out through the slit, demanding, "Land sakes, what is it, girl?"

"It's Thea! The baby. She's having it — *now!*"

"Be there in a jiff," Nelldean replied, then disappeared.

Breathing hard, Penny leaned against the wagon, weak with relief. "Thank God for Nelldean." Penny's confidence began to come back. An excitement began to surge through her. Maybe this would bring Thea back to life. With a new baby to care for, the future to think about, maybe things would work out. With God's help and Nelldean's faith and her own stubborn determination, they'd get through this somehow.

On their way back to the Sayres' wagon together, Nelldean assured Penny she had been a helper at a dozen or so birthings. "Thea's probably stronger than she looks. And she's young and has had one young'un already. Yes, I know it's sooner than expected, but maybe she miscalculated. That happens many a time. It'll be fine, God willin'."

The next few hours were a blur of following

Nelldean's instructions, bathing Thea's face with cool cloths, holding the hand she gripped so hard, whispering words of encouragement to her throughout the long night. Many times Penny was to repeat her grateful prayer for Nelldean's friendship, her calm presence beside her.

Penny wasn't sure when she became conscious of a change in Nelldean's manner. Alarmed, she turned to look at Nelldean, and she read something in the woman's face that turned her cold. "What is it? Is it taking too long?" Then she glanced back at Thea, who lay back against the pillows exhausted, her face chalky, with dark smudges of shadow underneath the closed eyes.

"I'm afraid the baby's dead," Nelldean said sadly. "Not moving, not at all."

A rush of anger, fear choked Penny. She looked down at Thea, her face a pale oval, the dark masses of hair tangled about it. There was a clamminess to her skin when Penny touched it with the dampened towel. *Oh, no, Lord, the baby might have saved Thea, might have —*

Dawn inched fingers of light through the gaping canvas flaps. Nelldean touched Penny's shoulder and whispered, "Maybe you better take Belinda over to our wagon, give her some breakfast. There's nothin' much more to do here but wait —"

"Let me stay, Nelldean. Belinda will go with you. She loves Nate. You're right. It might be better for her to not be here if —" Penny could not bring herself to say any more, for the lump rising in her throat felt as big and hard as a stone.

Nelldean nodded and stiffly moved to the end of the wagon and hefted the little girl down. Nelldean's leaving must have aroused Thea, for she opened her huge, shadowed eyes and at first seemed dazed. Then her gaze focused on Penny. She wet her parched and swollen lips with her tongue and in a raspy voice said, "Penny. Bend down. I can't talk any louder." Her thin fingers touched her throat. "Sore."

"Don't try to talk if it hurts."

"Have to. Something I must —"

Penny bent closer.

"Penny," Thea said again. "Promise me?"

"Yes, of course, whatever."

"Promise . . . ?"

"What do you want me to promise, Thea?"

With obvious effort, Thea swallowed and tried again. "Take care . . . Belinda?"

"Yes, of course, I will. We *both* will."

Thea made a motion as if to shake her head. She looked infinitely weary. Just then a wave of pain swept over her.

Fear gripped Penny. Where was Nelldean? Why didn't she come back? She didn't know what to do except hold Thea's hand, feeling the bite of her fingers and nails press deeply into the skin of her wrist.

"Please, Penny." Thea's eyes looked desperate. "There isn't time. If I don't . . . *you must —*"

"Don't say that, Thea. Don't even think it." Penny's voice choked.

Thea's eyes closed and Penny knew the end was near. Her friend could no longer hear her — would never hear her again.

Penny didn't remember how much later she had stumbled to the end of the wagon and hoarsely called Nelldean's name, knowing it was too late.

Other wagons were already astir with people at their morning duties, cooking fires were sending swirls up into the misty morning, and there was the usual clatter of kettles and frying pans. Penny was aware of voices, children's laughter. Everyone was going about their regular chores as if nothing terrible was happening. When the worst possible thing was happening. Thea's young life was ebbing out slowly, inevitably, irrevocably, just as her lifeblood was draining away and with her the little baby, who had never had a chance to live.

When it was all over, Penny knew Nelldean had done everything she could. Yet it had all been for nothing. Thea and the baby were gone.

Maybe there was no hope even from the beginning. Thea was too depleted in strength and will to live, the baby too small. There was nothing more to say. Nothing more to do. But to go on. Alone. Somehow.

Chapter 17

Penny huddled under her blanket. She couldn't stop shivering. Every once in a while a deep shudder shook the length of her body. It couldn't be true. It couldn't have happened. But it *was,* and it *had!* Thea was dead and the baby with her!

Nelldean had held Penny, who was wracked with sobs and clung to her. The older woman wisely let her cry until there seemed to be no tears left, then she said gently, "Maybe it's best this way, honey. I don't think the poor little thing wanted to live. Not after your brother died. The will just seemed to go right out of her. And the baby was just too tiny and too weak. . . ."

Was Nelldean right? Had Thea just given up? For the last few weeks, ever since Brad's drowning, there had been a kind of lostness about her. She had had to be reminded to eat, to respond. At the mention of Brad's name, her haunted eyes were always misty with tears ready to fall. She seemed enveloped in a web of grief from which she could not disentangle herself. She hardly noticed Belinda nor anything around her. It was as if her own spirit had departed with Brad.

Penny had never seen two people more in love than Thea and her brother. Only recently, at one of several impromptu weddings held among the wagon train folks — some on very short acquaintance and with little notice — Penny had made the comparison. At Thea and Brad's wedding, even in the inappropriate black dress mandated by her stepmother, Thea had been radiant. Her face, under the bonnet Grams had trimmed at the last minute with flowers and ribbons, was shining with happiness. Brad had been unable to take his eyes off his bride. As they repeated their vows, they had seemed oblivious to everyone else. Saying the words as they looked into each other's eyes brought tears to everyone else's. At that moment, Penny had determined she herself would never settle for anything less than that kind of love.

Brad and Thea had so much to look forward to together, with Belinda and a new baby. Now they were all gone! It was too cruel that all that love could end so tragically. The three of them had grown up together. Brad and Thea were part of everything Penny remembered about her childhood; she didn't have one memory that didn't include them in some way. She couldn't imagine what life would be like without them. Penny felt like a part of herself had been ripped away.

Thea had been her playmate, her companion, her confidante, her dearest friend. They had laughed together, cried together, prayed together, kept each others' secrets, shared the good, the bad, everything. How empty her world would be without Thea.

Penny stuffed an edge of her quilt into her mouth to stifle her sobs so as not to disturb Nelldean, who had stayed over with her and Belinda that night.

The next day as they buried Thea and the baby she had not lived long enough to name the air seemed filled with dust. The wind blew, constantly covering everything with a gritty mask, stinging the eyes, crawling down the backs of necks. Penny, standing motionless with Belinda in her arms, felt as though her heart would break. The wind tugged at her skirt and blew her hair into her eyes, which were already blinded with tears. Heartsick, she watched as the men shoveled the clumps of sandy earth over the shallow grave, then began covering it with rocks. Penny knew the reason for the rocks. Many times they had passed graves along the trail that had been dug out either by marauding Indians looking for clothes or jewelry or, worse still, by wild animals. The possibility of such a fate for Thea and her baby filled Penny with horror. The pain of leaving her dear ones in untended graves was intense.

The weight of Belinda's little body in her arms reminded her that she was not completely alone. She had a new and sacred responsibility. She was all the child had now. Belinda was an orphan: no mother, no father, no little brother or sister. Now what? *What shall I do?* echoed Penny's mind hollowly. Above all, she was determined not to give way to fear.

In the end, it was Nelldean who offered the answer to Penny's agonizing question. Fort Hall was the turn-off point; there the emigrants going to California would part with those heading for Oregon. To wait at Fort Hall for an escort back to Missouri seemed useless.

"Why not come to Oregon with us?" Nelldean urged. "We can join forces. You know how to drive a team; we can share provisions and supplies. Nate can help you with the animals, and I'll do the cookin' and help take care of Belinda. When we get to Oregon, you can sell your outfit, then decide what to do next."

It seemed the only sensible thing to do. The

decision was made. They went through the Sayres' wagon, taking what supplies were left, giving some things away to others who had less, moving a few possessions, and setting more along the wayside. Penny acted in a nearly automaton manner, motivated only by necessity. She still had not had time to fully grieve or to weigh all her new and enormous responsibilities.

In the days following Thea's burial, Penny's sorrow was too deep for tears then. Only later, sitting on the driver's seat, holding the reins as the weary team plowed on the increasingly difficult trail, did she let tears come. It had all turned out so differently from the high hopes and dreams the three of them had had starting out.

On those long, dusty days, she remembered all the glowing reports in the brochure articles, urging people to join the mighty emigrant movement west . . . they would be fulfilling the country's "manifest destiny." Had drowning been Brad's destiny? And a prairie grave for his widow and stillborn baby? Life seemed too cruel. Penny had never thought it would be like this. The great adventure was like ashes to her. Bitterly she asked herself, *What more could happen?*

What did happen was another stunning blow. Belinda stopped talking. In the midst of all her own indecision, her own uncertainty, preoccupied, distracted with everything that must be taken care of and decided, Penny did not notice it right away. Rather than the active little child who had been toddling about, chattering constantly, making up her own words for things in an attempt in real vocal communication, Belinda was suddenly mute. Penny could not be sure exactly when it had happened, but when she realized it, it came as a dreadful shock.

Panicked into action, Penny worked frantically to get her to talk again. She fashioned hand puppets from old stockings, making them dance and ask questions; she told stories by the hour, trying to get Belinda to guess the ending or say the names of the characters; she sang to her, hoping the little girl would join in as she used to love to do; but nothing worked. All her efforts, all the games she played trying to trick Belinda into some verbal reaction, were in vain. The child refused to speak. Whatever world into which she had retreated she could not explain, share, or talk about.

"I wish I knew what to do, Nelldean. That lost, longing look in her eyes is enough to break your heart."

"Well, all my life I've heard people say 'struck dumb,' " Nelldean replied. "I think that's what happened to Belinda. She was so frightened she was struck dumb. I believe, in time, she'll talk again. It's certainly not that she don't understand what's being said around her. You've seen the way her eyes follow you and how she turns her head from one or the other of us when we're talking?" Nelldean nodded her head sagely. "You'll see it'll happen one of these days. You've just got to be patient."

But Penny was impatient. She longed to have someone else take over the responsibility for Belinda, to tell her what to do. It was all almost too much to bear. Penny felt her energy drain away. What had happened to her? What had become of her original enthusiasm for the journey, her optimism at the start of each new day? As they neared Fort Hall, where the ones bound for California would leave the wagon train, Penny was wracked with memories of how Brad used to say that once they got to California, everything would be worth it. To him it was the fabled rainbow's end. Thea had been a reluctant traveler, and Belinda had not been asked if she wanted to come. Penny remembered how she herself had looked at it as a chance for adventure, an escape from a humdrum existence. She had loved the journey at first. She had felt free of all the restrictions, expectations, and the proscribed future her Dunwoodie girlfriends looked forward to

— having a husband and children, becoming a wife, keeping house, cooking, sewing, canning. She hadn't been ready for that . . . not yet. Not for a long time. The idea of independence had excited her imagination.

The irony was that instead of gaining freedom, she had gotten more responsibility than she had ever bargained for, with no one to help her carry the burden or share it with her.

Sometimes she felt like one of the Israelites wandering for forty years in the desert — except for *her* there was no pillar of cloud by day or moon by night, no manna, just day after grinding day, dust, heat, dryness, miles of parched grass stretching endlessly — a stark, cruel, yet somehow beautiful land.

Only by not trying to look ahead could Penny function at all. She tried to meet each day as it came, concentrating only on the task at hand. By not allowing herself to worry about the risks that still lay ahead, she could at least pretend they did not exist.

Caught up in each day's demands, her anxiety about Belinda hovered over her constantly. Would the little girl ever regain her speech? On the surface the child seemed much the same, though not smiling so readily. But there were no tantrums, no crying spells. She just didn't speak. If she missed her parents, there was no outward indication.

She did not ask about them. For the last few weeks of her mother's life, she had become used to Penny and Nelldean taking care of her. Nate was wonderful with her, taking her for rides on his shoulders and playing his harmonica for her.

In gratitude to both Nelldean and her grandson, Penny did more than her share of the work as the wagon train moved into the valley that would eventually lead them into the Oregon Territory. Work helped Penny suppress her gnawing worries. The days became a blur. At night she was too tired to do anything more than crawl into her bed at the back of the wagon and, with Belinda snuggled beside her, pray for the oblivion of sleep, the absence of nightmares. Then to wake and wearily and sadly begin another day.

Finally Nelldean took her to task. "Penny, you can't go on like this, girl. This is not the end of the road for you. Count your blessings. You're alive, number one. You're strong. You've come through a mighty hard time, but you did and you're stronger for it whether you realize it or not. And Belinda needs you. You're all she's got."

At Fort Hall Nate helped Penny unload more of the contents of Brad's wagon, and some of Thea's treasured furnishings had to be left there. If she was to do the driving for the rest of the way to Oregon, the weight for her already weary oxen had to be lightened. Penny kept only a few things that later Belinda might want of her mother's belongings. She added one more sad postscript to the letter she had written Grams to be sent from there:

I know it was Brad's dream to go to California. But there was no way I could persuade the wagon master to let me come with the part of the train headed there. I believe it was best for me to accept Nelldean and Nate's urging to join them. At least I will have the support of good friends until I know what I should do from there. Nelldean's faith had sustained me. As soon as we reach Oregon City, I will write again.

PART 4

Journey's End

Chapter 18

From Fort Hall Penny had sent the letter to Grams containing the tragic news of the deaths of Brad, Thea, and the baby. She knew what a bitter blow this would be to her grandmother, who had loved them all so dearly. But she also knew that Grams was brave and courageous, that she had known tragedy and loss before and survived. She would again. However, Penny was not as certain about her own ability to go on.

"Dearest Grams," Penny began her first letter from Oregon City,

Many times along the trail I wondered if our journey would ever end. Of course, I thought it would end in California, but here we are in Oregon. Main Street is an amazing mixture, with a variety of stores, saloons, boarding houses, more saloons, dance halls, a barber shop, a newspaper office, a general store, a doctor's office, a pharmacist, a dentist, a bank, a freight office, and who knows what else. Some of the buildings look flimsy, some well built.

I'm told that on some of the backstreets can be found some very nice frame houses with gardens — the residences of those who came here twenty years ago and established a town like the ones they left back east. Further out are ranches, cattle and horse farms, and miles and miles of orchards. Fruit grows plentifully here, especially a luscious kind of pear.

We are staying in the home of Bess Fulton, a friend of Nelldean's son and daughter-in-law. She has kindly offered us her hospitality, as she has three empty rooms. Her grown sons have gone to the California gold fields, and she says she is glad for the company.

I got a good price for our wagon, the two oxen, and the equipment. I kept Brad's horse, although he is worn from the long journey. Still, he is better than what I've seen for sale at the local livery stable. With some good feed and care, he should recover from any bad effects of the trip.

Now she paused in her letter. The hard part came next: to explain what had happened to Belinda in the aftermath of her parents' deaths, then ask if she should bring the little girl back to Dunwoodie as soon as she could arrange it. Unsure herself about what was the best thing to do, Penny needed Grams' good judgment. She finished the letter by assuring Grams that other than that, both she and Belinda were in good health, Oregon was beautiful, and she would await her answer. Penny took the letter to the post office and mailed it.

Grams' reply was a long time coming. Even though Nelldean told her it sometimes took months for letters to be received and answered, Penny became impatient. With every day that went by bringing no word from Grams, she grew more anxious. Was Grams ill? Was something wrong back home? Why hadn't she heard from her?

"I'm worried. Why hasn't she written?" Penny fretted to Nelldean after another futile trip to the post office. "I've got to do something, Nelldean. I can't expect Bess to put us up forever. I've got to make some money to travel on when I take Belinda back to Dunwoodie."

"Are you sure that's what you want to do, Penny? You and Belinda could stay here, make Oregon your home," Nelldean suggested mildly. "You know, you could file for a homestead yourself. Women out here have done that — many of them."

"A homestead? Me?" Penny looked surprised, then slowly shook her head. "I don't think so, Nelldean. I think when I hear from Grams, she'll tell me to bring Belinda back to Dunwoodie — *home*." But even as she said the word, Penny felt a strange detachment. Home? Somewhere along the trail, she had lost the sense of home.

In the meantime Penny tried to find some kind of work in case she needed to earn passage back east. However, there were dismayingly few opportunities for employment for young women. Some took in boarders, did laundry, or baked bread to make a living. But none of these was a possibility for her. Penny was discouraged, and her hope centered on a letter from Grams with some money for her to bring Belinda back to Dunwoodie.

A month, six weeks, went by and still no letter. Coming back from yet another disappointing trip to the post office one day, she met Nelldean's questioning glance with a shake of her head.

"Nothing! No letter, no job! I'm so depressed, Nelldean. I can't help it!"

"Somethin's bound to turn up, girl. Just you wait and see."

"You mean a miracle; that's what I need," Penny sighed.

"Then you'll get one," Nelldean said with

conviction. "You've just got to be patient, learn to wait for the Lord to act."

Nelldean sounded just like Grams, Penny thought nostalgically.

In the meantime at the beginning of November, the Oregon winter set in, with daily downpours. To Penny it seemed ironic that on the long, dusty trail they had thirsted for just one drop of water and here it seemed to do nothing but rain. On one such night, as the rain pounded like a drumbeat on the tin roof, Penny got out her Bible, searching for some encouraging passages to boost her flagging spirit. She remembered the desperate prayers she had prayed those nights, lying sleepless in the wagon. How she had dredged up fragments of Scripture from memory — "If you abide in me and my words abide in you, you shall ask what you will —" Had they been mindless, meaningless? Or was what the Bible promised true? Penny closed her eyes, clenched her fists. *Yes, I do believe. God will show me the way — the right way.*

Somehow she got through Christmas. Nelldean and Bess made a great occasion of it, and Belinda was the beneficiary of their love and talents. Knitted caps, scarves, and mittens. A rag doll with yellow yarn hair and a wardrobe of dresses and bonnets. Nate had built a small wooden cradle for it as well.

They all attended church service in the morning (there were as many churches in Oregon City as saloons). Afterward they had a festive dinner with duck — Nate's contribution — creamed onions, vegetables, mashed potatoes, and three kinds of pie: mince, apple, pumpkin. Beneath all the gaiety, the laughter and fun, Penny felt a tinge of loneliness. Nelldean and Bess had done their best, but Oregon City wasn't home. Who would ever have thought she would be homesick for Dunwoodie?

Nelldean had been right. In January came the long-delayed letter from Grams, along with a much battered box containing Christmas gifts for them all. Penny tore open the envelope addressed to her at general delivery in Grams' familiar handwriting. Her eyes raced down the closely written page. But the letter did not contain what Penny had hoped nor what she had expected. She read it with a growing feeling of dismay.

Somewhere in the second paragraph, she read the news that Todd had married. It was like a jolt. She was surprised to realize that somewhere hovering in the back of her mind had been the thought that when she *did* return to Dunwoodie with Belinda, Todd would be there, still in love with her, still wanting to marry, and that together they might make a home for Belinda. She hadn't thought this out in any great detail; it had just been there. Just as Todd had always been there in her life, patient, caring, kind — waiting. Well, that wasn't the case now. It surprised her that she felt so let down, as unfair of her as that was. She had never given him any reason to hope. In fact, she had done everything to discourage him. Why should she feel betrayed?

Maybe this was all part of *really* growing up — to realize that nothing stays the same. Everything changes. *Her* circumstances, *her* life had. *She* certainly had. She was no longer the girl who had left Dunwoodie. Nor was she still the girl Todd had loved and wanted to marry.

Penny found other surprises in the letter. It seemed that Cousin Sara and Tom and their little Jenny had moved into the house to live with Grams. Her grandmother wrote,

It's such a comfort to have them here. I wouldn't have told you for the world, but I was right lonely after the four of you left. Even Uncle Billy was lonesome for young folks — especially a baby. But Sara and Tom are as lively as can be, and we all have a great time together. They're expecting another baby in the spring, so we shall have a full house, but the more the merrier, I always say.

Except there's no room anymore for me, Penny thought. Her tears blurred her eyes as she read Grams' final paragraph:

You have Belinda to raise now. Why this should be, why this has come about, we will find out someday. God works in mysterious ways, as we all know. It would be foolhardy for you to attempt the long trip back here to bring Belinda back. To what? You have friends who love you, a new life ahead of you, Penny. I'm sure all the things I tried to teach you and Brad will stand you in good stead. You will always be in my loving prayers, and I know God will guide and protect you in all you do.

Penny reread the letter. In little less than a year since she'd been gone, Todd had found someone else, and Grams had taken on a new family to nurture and love. Her first reaction was hurt. Her throat felt sore with the effort not to cry.

Quickly she blinked back the telling tears. She was just being selfish, self-indulgent. She *should* be happy for Grams, happy for Todd. And she *was*.

★ ★ ★

That night as Penny got Belinda ready for bed she took the little girl onto her lap and hugged her. "It's going to be all right, honey. Things are going to be fine — just fine," she whispered, wishing she fully believed that herself.

Now that there was no going home, she knew it was up to her to find some kind of work and to make a home for Belinda. How that would be done, she had no idea. That miracle Nelldean had promised she'd get seemed far away.

At the end of February and in the first week of March signs of spring could definitely be seen and felt. With the arrival of the new season, Penny resolved to accept what had happened, make the best of it, build a life for herself and Belinda here in Oregon. First she had to find some way to support them both. Nelldean had told her she'd get her "miracle." And one day she did.

Oregon City was growing constantly. Main Street was being extended, with new buildings going up every day. New businesses were opening up: a millinery, a dress shop, a hardware store. Maybe she could get a job as a clerk in one of them. She wrote a neat hand, was good at sums. She walked along the wooden boardwalk, glancing from one side of the street to the other. Just then, passing Miller's General Mercantile, she saw a sign in the window: BOOK AGENTS WANTED.

She halted. What did that mean? What was a book agent? A sales person? There was only one way to find out: go in and ask. Penny straightened her shoulders, took a deep breath, opened the door, and walked inside.

"Mr. Miller?" she tentatively addressed the man behind the counter, who stood near an impressive silver cash register.

"The same. Speaking," he said, regarding her with both curiosity and admiration. Not often did such an attractive young woman, neatly dressed in bonnet and gloves, come into the store.

"My name is Penny Sayres, and I've newly arrived in Oregon City. I came in with the wagon train," she added, to let him know she was strong, hardy, and able to work hard. "I'm staying with Mrs. Fulton, and I'm looking for work. I wondered — the sign in the window says book agents wanted — do you ever hire women as agents?"

Mr. Miller gave her a long, astonished look. But he'd always liked a woman with spunk and determination. He nodded his head as he spoke: "I don't know why not. Books is books. Readin' is readin'. The only question is can you sell? Agents get paid a sum for every book order they take, plus a percentage of the cover cost of the book. Don't matter who sells 'em. Do you have transportation? A small buggy or wagon? You may have to go quite a distance to peddle 'em. There's lots of women in ranches in the outlying districts who could use this here fine book." He picked up a large volume displayed on the counter and held it up so Penny could read the title. "It's called *Handbook for Housewives: A Complete Guide to the Art of Creating a Harmonious Home, a Happy Husband, and Healthy Children.*"

Penny felt something click inside. Of course she could do it. "A woman selling to women might be even better," she said almost breathlessly.

Mr. Miller's eyes twinkled, he nodded in approval. "Fine and dandy. You're hired." He then proceeded to pack a box of books and handed her a ledger to write up her sales. "There you go, Miss Sayres."

Lugging an armful of books and a sales ledger, Penny hurried home.

"Nelldean, I've got a job!" she called as she entered the house. Nelldean and Bess were in the kitchen where they were feeding Belinda. All three looked expectantly at Penny as she came through the door.

In a rush she told them what had come

about. Nelldean looked pleased, even a bit smug. "You got your miracle then, didn't you?" she asked Penny.

Penny laughed.

Bess chimed in, "Well, it's sure better than doing laundry or housework and probably pays more."

"The man at the store said I can make as much as I'm willing to work at it. I'll have to rent a small buggy to make my rounds. Mr. Miller says most of my customers will probably be ranch wives on places that are located quite a distance from town. Will that cost much, do you think?" she asked Bess, who had lived in town a long time.

"Try Hiram's Livery and tell them Bess Fulton sent you. They knew my husband Jake real well. I think they'll give you a fair price."

At Nelldean's suggestion, Penny sold some of the equipment from Brad's wagon that they had stored in Bess's barn after Nate took what he needed for his homestead. She rented a small rig and a horse with that sum, which, the livery owner agreed, could be applied to their purchase if she wanted to later.

Penny was excited at the prospect of her new career. Her old enthusiasm for adventure returned, and she was determined to make a success of it. She knew enough about horses to select an older one, but he was healthy, mild natured, and in good shape. The small buggy was just right for one driver and a box of books on the seat beside her.

She had moderate success selling the book in town, although at first some women looked askance at her, with suspicion or condescension. The book, however, sold itself on most occasions. It was the kind of book that had wide appeal for women, especially women far from homes back east who were struggling to build a home in the new country, in the desolate mining communities, on isolated ranches and farms, as well as in town. Many of the women had no family or friends.

Although she obviously preferred to be with Penny, Belinda stayed with Nelldean when Penny left each morning. Both Bess and Nelldean doted on the little girl, and Penny was grateful for this and for her job. Soon she would be able not only to contribute to the household expenses and pay a small board and room to Bess, but eventually have enough money to take Belinda back to Dunwoodie.

Penny always had stories to recount when she returned home in the evenings after a day of selling. Nelldean and Bess took great interest in her adventures as a book saleslady. It also gave them many a laugh, for Penny was a good mimic, regaling them with tales of her experiences, some intimidating, some funny, some exasperating. After a few ludicrous trial attempts, Penny got better at her sales "spiel" and much more confident in her new role.

Penny's life was busy with her responsibilities and with the important decisions she was mulling over. She was seriously weighing Nelldean's advice and praying hard for some direct answers. She recalled Grams saying, "God don't play guessing games. If you want to know something, ask him." Maybe that was easy for Grams, who had had a long, close relationship with the Lord. But Penny was afraid her own had been sporadic, her entreaties being more the quick, desperate kind.

With new resolution, she did begin to seek his direction, reading her Bible every night before going to bed. As she searched the pages for wisdom and understanding she was sure Nelldean had given her wise counsel but that it was up to her to understand, to really know if this was what she should do. Would it really be best for her and Belinda to stay here and build a life for themselves thousands of miles from their nearest family? After all, Thea's stepmother was still alive and Penny's grandmother and her cousins and Uncle Billy too. Would it be better to go back, where they would be surrounded by old friends and where maybe a doctor could help Belinda regain her speech? Torn by indecision, Penny would look over at Belinda, sleeping curled up, one rosy cheek cradled in a chubby hand sleeping dreamlessly. The road ahead seemed shadowed, winding into the distance she could not see. Night after night she sought and prayed for an answer.

After counting up her receipts one evening she announced proudly to Nelldean, "Well, if this keeps up, I'll soon have enough money to take Belinda home."

She and Nelldean were sitting at the kitchen table having a cup of coffee together after supper. Bess had gone to her Wednesday night prayer meeting, and the two of them were alone.

"Are you still sure that's what you want to do, Penny?"

"I don't know what else to do, Nelldean. I keep thinking Belinda needs to have a family. Grams adores her and there's Uncle Billy and. . . ." Her voice trailed off uncertainly. "Shouldn't she be brought up near her family?"

"But you said Thea had no blood relatives, didn't you? Only a stepmother that she was never close to? You and your brother were or-phans and your grandmother's over sixty? What would you be taking her back to?"

Nelldean's words struck a deep chord of truth — a truth Penny had not really considered too closely — maybe because she didn't want to.

"When it comes right down to it, Penny, you're all Belinda *really has,*" Nelldean reminded her gently.

"Except *you.*" Penny reached across the table and patted Nelldean's hand. "She couldn't have anyone more loving than you to take care of her."

"Yes, I do love her like she was my own," Nelldean agreed. "But I'm past fifty and can't go on forever. You need to be thinking about the future, yours and Belinda's. Of course, someday I hope you'll marry. Find a man who will be a good provider, a loving companion — a good father. But until then — the best thing a woman can do is to act like she may not find someone to her liking. To make her own way, provide for herself."

"I'm trying my best, Nelldean. It's hard work and slow, trying to earn enough to support us both."

"I know, honey, and that's why I'm going to suggest what I've been thinkin'. There's opportunities out here in the West for a woman alone — even a woman with a child. Land, for one. Maybe you ought to consider adopting Belinda legally. That way you could file a claim for a homestead as head of a household. It would be a security for the two of you for the future."

"Homestead by myself?" Penny's voice expressed her uncertainty. "But what would *I* do with all that acreage, Nelldean?"

"There's different size parcels, I think. And you could always sell off some, if it came to that. All it takes to meet the requirements is putting up some kind of a shelter or shack. I'd help and Nate would too. Little by little you could build on it, plant a garden, grow vegetables, live on it at least part of the year. And you could do that while building. You've had experience roughin' it on the trail. You're a capable gal! I seed that with my own eyes."

"I don't know, Nelldean," Penny said doubtfully.

"Well, think about it. If you decide to give up goin' back east, that is. But don't take too long, Penny. More and more emigrants are coming every day. Pretty soon land is goin' to get scarce and expensive as more people pour into the territory. Now's the time."

In the days that followed, Penny thought a great deal about Nelldean's suggestion. She respected her wisdom and knew Nelldean was giving her this good advice with the best intentions and for what she thought was Penny's own good. But it seemed such a big step to take, an irrevocable one. . . . File for a homestead? It sounded frightening.

Chapter 19

After a few months of selling, Penny gained more confidence and self-assurance and felt she was doing reasonably well. Of course, there were bad days, when most of the answers had been noes mixed with a few curt rebuffs. On one such day, Penny was tempted to return home for the rest of the afternoon. The day was warm and she was tired and thirsty, but because she was determined not to end the day with no sales, she decided to try a new route, hoping she would have better luck. Taking a rutted country road from town, she soon found herself out in the rolling countryside.

When she saw a house on a hilltop at the end of a long, curving lane, she slowed her horse to a walk and read the sign on the rail fence: L. C. BOUDREY. Perhaps here she would find a lonely ranch wife who was eager for some company and who could easily be persuaded to buy one of her books. She might even be offered a glass of cool water or lemonade, she thought.

The gate stood open, so Penny turned in

and rode up to the house, a rustic, well-built log-and-stone building. At one side was a corral with four sleek horses, on the other side was a nice vegetable garden with some flowers at the edge. *Uh-huh*, Penny said to herself, *a very good prospect indeed! Prosperous rancher, a wife who takes pride in her home. What could be better?*

Penny got out of her buggy, hitched the horse under a shade tree away from the corral so that he wouldn't spook the other horses. Then she picked up her satchel of books and her order pad and walked toward the house. Before she reached it, the front door opened, and a man stepped out onto the porch.

Penny halted, momentarily taken aback. She hadn't expected a man. Her second thought was that he didn't look like a rancher — at least, he wasn't dressed like one. He had on a striped shirt, the sleeves rolled up to the elbows, a brown vest, dark pants, and riding boots. As she tried to regain her poise, she wracked her brain: what kind of man would be home in the middle of the day? A teacher, a preacher? Someone who worked nights? A *gambler* in one of the saloons that lined Main Street? She fervently hoped not.

When he took a few steps to the edge of the porch, she got a better look at him. He was above average height and leanly built. He had a thin face with high cheekbones, a strong nose, and deep set eyes. Although somewhat flustered by his appearance, Penny quickly composed herself. Smiling pleasantly, she began her pitch, with a slightly altered opening: "Good afternoon, sir."

"Good afternoon," he replied, folding his arms he leaned against one of the porch posts regarding her quizzically.

"Mr. Boudrey, I presume? L. C. Boudrey?"

"The same," he said with a slight smile.

"May I introduce myself?" Penny continued. "I am a representative of the Addington Publishing Company. May I speak to the lady of the house?"

He shook his head. "No, ma'am, I'm sorry, but you may not."

His response startled her, but she attempted not to show it as she wondered, *Good heavens, why ever not?* Was his wife ill? Does he not allow her to speak to strangers? Or something more bizarre? Has he kept her prisoner?

Redirecting her random thoughts back to her purpose of making a sale, Penny determined not to be so easily defeated. After all, she had ridden out of her way to get here — she was not about to give up without making an effort. All the sales manuals advised making at least three tries to close a sale. Penny took a deep breath and another tack.

"Then may I make an appointment for another time? I believe I have something that will be of great interest to her and also bring happiness to *you* as well."

"Oh?" the man lifted an eyebrow. "How do you mean?"

Just then an errant wind arose, lifting Penny's bonnet so that it fell back from her head. As it dangled for a moment by its ribbons, he caught a glimpse of her coppery hair gleaming in the sunlight. Before she righted it, L. C. Boudrey saw the face that had at first been half hidden by the shadow of the brim. He saw there was a drift of golden freckles across a charmingly tilted nose, and her eyes were slate blue and her candid expression was earnest.

Penny made a quick grab for her bonnet, setting it straight again, and without missing a beat went right on talking. "I have a volume that is indispensable to every household. Indeed, sir, I can guarantee there are at least thirty suggestions that will provide this home with a new atmosphere of comfort, cleanliness, convenience, congeniality, competence, composure as well as new health, heartiness, habits to ensure energy, effectiveness, and enlightenment."

Encouraged that he seemed to be listening

intently, Penny increased her momentum. "This book, which I am offering homemakers for a ridiculously low down payment, payable in three easy monthly installments, will enrich the life of this entire household. It contains sound, practical advice on nutrition, innovative ideas to insure a happy, healthy environment. It includes many Scriptural quotations, beautifully printed at the beginning of each section applicable to the subject. These are under the headings of menus, medicinal remedies, food preparation, sewing tips, decoration for each room of the house, care of babies, domestic pets, and how to remove every kind of spot or spill. This is the complete household-management tool. It is an indispensable resource for every homemaker. . . ." She paused before making her best closing plea: "Could I not be allowed to present to your wife this wonderful compendium of reference for every possible circumstance or condition a housewife might encounter in the course of her daily life?"

"No ma'am. Regretfully, I'm afraid not."

Again Penny was astonished. She had thought she was making all her points and that he was receptive. To be turned down not only disappointed her, but she could not guess why. Hadn't she perfected her "sales pitch," achieved a persuasive approach, practicing it endlessly for a patient Nelldean? She *knew* she had done an excellent job. Why was this man refusing even to allow her to show and explain it to his wife?

Bewilderment made her bold, and Penny asked, "May I ask *why* you want to withhold this treasure of information from the lady of the house?"

That trace of amusement in his eyes moved to his mouth and he smiled almost apologetically. "Because, simply stated, there *is* no lady of the house. I am — alas — not married."

Caught completely off guard by this statement, Penny took a step back, embarrassed. Then suspecting he had led her on intentionally, she drew herself up in dignified indignation and retorted, "Well then! Since you're a *bachelor,* living alone, *you* could probably make good use of the contents of this book *yourself!*"

At this the man threw back his head and laughed heartily. In spite of herself, Penny began to laugh too. Then he said, "I'm sorry. Do forgive me. I didn't mean to purposely mislead you. But you must admit — there was no stopping you once you got started!" He took a clean white linen handkerchief from his vest pocket, wiped his eyes, and smiled broadly as he reached for his wallet. "And *of course,* I want to buy one of those marvelous books! You've convinced me. I'm sure it *is* something *no* household should be without," he mimicked her description. "How much?"

The transaction was made. The book changed hands as Penny assured him that it would live up to its promises. Reasserting her professional posture, she walked briskly back to her buggy and climbed in. Without looking back at the man on the porch, who was still watching her, she turned horse and buggy around and headed out the gate and back up the road.

All the way back into town, Penny considered the incident. Used to the rough, rugged, unschooled frontier types that populated the town, coming upon someone like L. C. Boudrey was a pleasant shock. Everything about him was different: his manners, his speech — even though he was dressed casually, his clothes were good quality. His attitude was self-confident yet courteous. And obviously he had a keen sense of humor! Ruefully she recalled how he seemed to enjoy teasing her.

That evening after supper Penny sat at the kitchen table, going over her order book. On Saturdays she took in her receipts and collected her payment from Mr. Miller for the week's sales. Overall, she had done fairly well this past week; the last sale of the day, to L. C.

Boudrey, had brought her total to the highest in any week so far.

Studying his signature on her copy of the sales slip, Penny knew it to be the fine penmanship of an educated man. What was such a man doing living alone on an isolated ranch? He was hardly a typical rancher, but she had yet to see a better homestead. She had caught a glimpse of a young orchard behind the house. The man certainly knew how to farm; still, she was curious about him. But then, she had found that all sorts of people had come out west for all sorts of reasons, none the same.

Like *herself*, for instance. She sighed. Someone else's decision had brought *her* here. Now it was up to her to make a go of it. Nelldean's repeated suggestion that she apply for a homestead kept coming back to her. Maybe she really *could.* Make a real home for herself and Belinda. She'd come this far — with God's help — so why not?

The only troubling part was that even though Nelldean constantly reassured her that someday it would just happen, Belinda still refused to talk. Maybe a homestead would be the answer. If they were settled on their own, maybe then Belinda would feel secure enough and become again the normal child she had been. Penny prayed earnestly that she would be shown clearly if this is what she should do.

Only a week or so later it seemed she got her answer, in the form of a means of additional income. When Penny went into Miller's Mercantile to get a new supply of books, Mr. Miller greeted her with the question, "What would you think of adding some new items to your line?"

"It depends on what they are," she answered cautiously. She wasn't yet so sure of her sales technique that she was ready to try to close one sale with the offer of something else.

Mr. Miller held up two engravings, one of Ulysses S. Grant and one of Robert E. Lee, suitable for framing.

"Take your pick," he said with a twinkle in his eyes. "American heroes both." He grinned. "Dependin' which side of the fence you're on."

Penny studied the two portraits for a moment, then said, "I'll take three of each. Let the customers decide which one they want."

Sales of the engravings were brisk. Westerners, Penny discovered, were patriotic and, whichever man they preferred, easily swayed by political persuasion and past regional loyalty. The engravings became a popular item.

Some customers even purchased *both!* By the middle of the week, she had already made more than any previous week.

Chapter 20

Penny's spirits were high. The books were selling well, and with the added commodity of the engravings, her nest egg was building up beyond the modest hopes she'd had when she started.

"I knew you could do it," Nelldean told her. "Now, what's keeping you from going ahead and getting you a homestead?"

"You know, Nelldean, I think you're right. Maybe I'll just do it."

It was a Saturday morning bright with sunshine, not a cloud in the sky, and Penny was preparing to go downtown to pick up her week's wages from Mr. Miller. She was taking Belinda with her as a special treat.

"Good girl!" Nelldean said approvingly as she tied Belinda's bonnet strings and gave the little girl a kiss. "Have a nice time, you two," she called after them as hand in hand they went out the door.

As Penny came down Main Street she saw a tall man striding down the opposite sidewalk. She thought there was something familiar about him, and then she recognized him. It was the rancher to whom she'd sold a book a few weeks before. She watched him as he stopped, unlocked the door, and went into one of the buildings across the street. It was then that she noticed the small sign: ATTORNEY AT LAW. He was a lawyer! No wonder he didn't look like a rancher.

Penny went on into the mercantile. Mr. Miller was leaning on the counter perusing a mail-order catalog when she came inside. He glanced up and, seeing Belinda was with her, greeted them both warmly.

"Well, good morning, ladies! And how's that pretty little miss today? Looks like you might need somethin' sweet. Maybe a licorice stick? Is that all right with Auntie?" He looked at Penny for permission. "Shall we let her choose for herself?"

Penny smiled and nodded and let Belinda toddle over to the candy case. Putting two chubby hands on the glass, she stared in for a few seconds, then shyly pointed to a twisted pink-and-white peppermint stick.

Over her head he whispered the words, "Not talking yet, eh?"

Since they had become good friends Penny had confided her concerns about Belinda. She shook her head and said, "We're hoping it will happen soon."

He got out the candy and handed it to the

little girl, then went over to the cash register and opened up the cash drawer. Penny followed him over to the counter.

"You know, her parents are both dead, and I'm thinking of adopting Belinda. I might be needing some legal assistance. Could you suggest someone trustworthy?"

"Boudrey," he said. "Couldn't find no finer fella than L. C. Boudrey. Smart as they come, but nice and as friendly as kin, what with all his ed'cation. To see him now you'd never have knowed how he looked when he first come here. Thin as a rail, he was. Pale as a ghost. He was in right poor health. Sent out here by his doctor for his health is what I heard. Mebbe to die? But before long he was fit as a fiddle. All this pure air, and workin' his ranch, goin' fishin' and ridin' his horses is just what he needed," Mr. Miller chuckled. "Jest what the doctor ordered, as they say. Anyways, after a while he opened his law office. 'Fore that nobody knowed he was a lawyer and all. No siree." Mr. Miller began counting out her money. "Well, now, here you are, Miss Sayres. You know, I'm thinking, come spring, we might add some other items to your wares. You've done mighty good selling, so there's no limit to what we could offer your customers. Might have to get you a bigger buggy —"

"That sounds interesting, Mr. Miller." Penny tucked the little roll of bills into her purse. "Thank you and thanks for the recommendation of the lawyer — Mister . . . ah, Mister . . ."

"Boudrey, L. C."

"Thanks," Penny said again. "Come, Belinda." She took the little girl's hand and left the store, feeling just a bit guilty for having rather deviously satisfied her own curiosity about the puzzling man she had met on her sales circuit.

From his office, L. C. Boudrey saw Penny coming out of Miller's Mercantile. He got up from his desk and went to the window. Ever since that day she had appeared at his ranch so unexpectedly, he had thought about her, wondered about her, hoped to see her again. He had not wanted to start tongues wagging in this small town by making direct inquiries about her, and so she remained a mystery. Usually he did not come into town on weekends; there was so many chores, work to do on his place. But today he had come in to go over some papers dealing with a land sale. This seemed like too lucky a coincidence to pass up.

He reached for his hat and was out the door within a minute. She was standing directly across the street when L. C. noticed the little girl with her and the striking resemblance between them. His heart sank. She must be married. And that was her child? Why was she working so hard as a book agent? So eager to make a sale? Could she be a widow? Or was her husband away at the gold fields? Many a gold-hungry man left wife and children behind. Like a good lawyer, he looked for evidence before coming to a conclusion. And as a lawyer, he had learned to be discreet. Still, he was determined to find out her status or stop thinking about her. He crossed the street.

"Hello, there," he greeted her, feeling foolish that he could not address her by her name, married or single. He blamed himself for feeling awkward. He should have looked at the sales slip for the book that was still in his waistcoat pocket. He had been so taken by her winsomeness, the very novelty of her occupation, so preoccupied by her selling ability that somehow her name had not even seemed important. More fool he!

Penny looked at him for a long moment before answering. It seemed uncanny that she had just found out all about him from Mr. Miller, and then suddenly there he was.

Mistaking her disconcerted expression for one of nonrecognition, Boudrey's self-confidence was jolted. She seemed to be trying to place him. With dismay he thought she did not even remember *him*, while *she* had made such an unforgettable impression on him.

Anxious to jog her memory and make a connection, he blurted out, "The book is most helpful. It certainly is everything you said it was . . . I'm very pleased I bought it —" Surreptitiously he glanced at her left hand to check for a wedding ring. But the little girl was holding it, and he could not see. "Yes, indeed, most pleased, Mrs. . . . ? Miss . . . ?"

"Sayres," Penny supplied the last name but not the title, so he was as much in the dark as ever. He tried again.

"And who is this pretty little lady?"

"This is Belinda," Penny answered, not thinking to identify the girl as her niece.

Frustrated, Boudrey shifted from one foot to the other and twisted the hat he had removed upon greeting her.

"I'm glad the book is proving helpful, Mr. Boudrey," Penny said and moved aside as if to go on.

Frantic to elicit more information, L. C. did not step aside. Instead he attempted to prolong the encounter. "Lovely day, isn't it? A good one to be out and about canvassing, I expect. I am sure there is a ready market for your estimable product." For once, his lawyer's fluency with words failed him and he came to a floundering stop.

Penny hesitated. Should she remind him this was Saturday, tell him she did not work on the weekends? Perhaps she should mention the engravings? He might buy one or both for his office. No, that would be too pushy. Suddenly Penny felt awkward. Was she getting a sales person's mentality?

Boudrey misinterpreted her silence as he made another futile attempt to discover her real situation. "It was very pleasant to see you. I hope we will meet again." *And often,* he added mentally.

Penny merely smiled and murmured, "That's probably possible," and she walked past him, adding, "Good day, Mr. Boudrey."

Watching her slim figure move gracefully down the wooden sidewalk, L. C. inwardly questioned his failure. Why had he not somehow persisted in discovering if she were married? Perhaps he might have asked after her husband's health in some subtle manner? If she had none, then he could possibly have asked if he might call on her? L. C. derided his own ineptness. At least he knew her name was Sayres and the little girl's name was Belinda. Nothing more.

Dejectedly, L. C. returned to his office.

Seeing her for the second time increased the interest she had evoked at the first one. Her cheeks were a becoming pink from the wind, her blue eyes bright, strands of coppery hair had escaped from the rim of her bonnet and curled fetchingly about her face. But there was more than physical attractiveness about her. There was intelligence and sensitivity in her expression, forthrightness in her manner, candor in the beautiful clear eyes. Instinctively he knew there was much more to this lady than met the eye. But how could he get to know her better without being unseemly? Social protocol was not as rigidly adhered to out here as back east. Still, it was clear to see that Miss (Mrs.?) Sayres had a natural refinement, a reticence that precluded any action on his part that might appear crude or indicate that he had taken too much for granted on such slight acquaintance.

Chapter 21

After that Saturday, Penny and L. C. Boudrey encountered each other often enough for it to be more than coincidence. At least on his part. Since the windows of his office fronted Main Street and were directly opposite Miller's Mercantile, the occasions Penny went there for her books or engravings also seemed the same time Boudrey had the urgent need to purchase something at the general store.

They always exchanged greetings and a few pleasantries, but since Penny was usually in a hurry to start her day of making sales calls, these meetings were brief.

However, the day Penny finally filed for a homestead at the city hall, she met L. C. just as she was coming down the courthouse steps, the papers in her hand.

In a burst of spontaneous excitement she told him what she had just done. He seemed genuinely enthusiastic about her decision.

"Well, it's a big step, I know," she said impulsively, "and one I wouldn't have undertaken without a lot of urging from Nelldean and Bess, to say nothing of beseeching the Lord to be a 'light onto my path'!" Then she stopped suddenly, feeling self-conscious. Maybe L. C. wasn't a religious man and wouldn't understand her frame of reference.

To her surprise he responded, "Nothing of importance should be undertaken *without* all those things: good advice of friends and people you trust, and prayer. I've seen too many people rush into big decisions without due consideration and deliberation, to say nothing of seeking providential guidance," he said, adding, "marriage being one of the main ones. Even Shakespeare cautioned against that in his most romantic of plays, *Romeo and Juliet* — what he said is applicable even today. People take on the responsibilities of marriage many times 'unadvisedly, suddenly, too like summer lightening.' " He paused, looking a bit embarrassed. "I apologize, Miss Sayres, I am too loquacious. A trait of lawyers, I'm afraid. Forgive me."

"There's nothing to forgive, Mr. Boudrey. I'm impressed by your familiarity with Shakespeare and how it applies to life. I've witnessed just such occasions of which you speak. On the journey west in our wagon train, there were several of those sudden marriages. An itinerant preacher would happen along, going back east mostly, and couples who hadn't said much more than 'howdy' to each other before decided that while he was there they might as well get married. I know Nelldean used to shake her head over them, saying she hoped that once those couples settled down, their marriages would prove to have been 'made in heaven,' not on the Oregon Trail!"

They both laughed and L. C. remarked, "Mrs. Hardison is both wise and witty."

"Yes. I rely on her advice and good sense," Penny said. Remembering Nelldean's most recent advice about adopting Belinda, Penny started to broach the subject, thinking L. C. could probably tell her what had to be done legally.

But before she could, he surprised her by asking, "Where is your sweet little daughter today? It is certainly inspiring to see such devotion between mother and child."

"You mean Belinda?" Penny asked. "But I'm not her mother. She's my niece, Mr. Boudrey. You see, my brother and sister-in-law, Belinda's parents, both perished on the way here. Our original destination was California. But after their deaths — well, it wasn't possible for me to go on alone. Nelldean kindly invited us to join her and Nate in their wagon. That's how we happened to come to Oregon."

L. C.'s spirits soared. Although he felt a

natural sympathy for the tragic circumstances Penny had just explained, he could not deny the truth. At last, to know that Penny was neither a married woman nor a widow but a single lady caring for an orphaned niece was good news indeed. His admiration for her fortitude and generosity skyrocketed. Recovered from his relief, L. C. intended to ask another question, but Penny said, "It was nice to see you again, Mr. Boudrey."

He quickly rejoined, "And a pleasure to see you again, *Miss* Sayres. Do give my kindest regards to Mrs. Hardison, won't you?"

"Mrs. Hardison? You've met Nelldean?"

"Yes, we were introduced by the Reverend Mr. McCall, with whom I happened to be conversing the other day when she happened along. She was kind enough to invite me to call. I hope that meets with your approval?"

Penny concealed her amusement but thought, *That sly boots, Nelldean! Always "Johnny on the spot," wasn't she? And never a word about the invitation!* Of course, L. C. Boudrey was not only a prosperous lawyer and rancher — handsome and personable — but he was also the perfect candidate, in Nelldean's opinion, of the *"someday"* husband and father for Belinda she was always assuring Penny would come along.

Suppressing a smile, Penny replied demurely, "Why, of course, Mr. Boudrey." They parted at the post office, and Penny went on her way, planning to gently chide Nelldean about her matchmaking.

Dearest Grams,

I don't know whether or not you will be surprised at the action I have just taken. I have embarked on a great adventure! "Another one?" I can see you now saying, shaking your head as you read this letter. I think you will agree it is a wise decision, considering Belinda and I are now out here, I have a well-paying job, good, faithful friends who care for us both and support my action. As of yesterday, I am a homesteader. It is what Brad wanted to do, and in a way I am doing it for him and for his daughter. It will one day belong to Belinda.

It is getting to be spring now and Oregon is very beautiful. The land I've filed for is next to Nelldean's grandson Nate's. He stayed on his land all winter even when it snowed and he now has a nice building, a barn and plans to raise a dairy herd. On the other side of my claim is land owned by a local lawyer.

Here Penny paused and thought about

L. C. Boudrey. Since Nelldean's none-too-subtle invitation, he had become a frequent visitor. The first time he had arrived at the house, he came, as Nate put it, "loaded for bear." He carried two bouquets, one for Nelldean, the other for Bess, both of which he presented with a flourish, as well as a box of chocolates for Penny and a shiny red top for Belinda.

Mindful of their conversation about his familiarity with Shakespeare, Penny had to bite her tongue not to tease him by quoting, "Beware of the Greeks when they come bearing gifts." She didn't want to make him feel uncomfortable when he was obviously trying to make a good impression.

Penny had to admit he was an excellent conversationalist. It was wonderful to have someone who had such a wealth of knowledge without being pompous or the least arrogant. He could also laugh and talk on plenty of mundane subjects. He discussed ranching with Nate and even got down on the floor to spin the top for Belinda.

Although Nelldean and Bess always tactfully disappeared at intervals during Mr. Boudrey's visits, Belinda was their constant chaperone. Because Penny's work kept her away most days, when she was at home, Belinda hardly let Penny out of her sight.

Penny knew Nelldean was hoping the friendship would turn into courtship, but Penny wasn't at all sure how she felt about L. C. Boudrey's attentions. She had so much on her mind these days: Belinda, first and foremost, and all that lay ahead of her on their homestead. Putting all these random thoughts aside, Penny went back to her letter to Grams.

When it gets to be summer, we will spend more time out there. Nate has promised to help me with the building that has to be erected on the property, and we'll probably spend the nights there while the weather is still fine. It will be a grand place for Belinda to play. I know you may feel some caution about what I've done, Grams — a woman alone with a small child. But really, things are different out here. Women have a great deal more independence. So many women are widows, having survived the long journey west but having lost their husbands on the way. There was much sickness — both cholera and smallpox — in our wagon train, taking a toll on those who had not been vaccinated. I see all around me women who have taken bold steps to support themselves and their children, opening boarding houses, restaurants, businesses of all kinds. There is a spirit here I cannot exactly explain; it's as if the ones who made it all the way out here are going to stay — not only "make the best of it" but to make the *most* of it.

Nelldean has been a wonderful support. She could not be more generous, caring, helpful if we were her own blood kin. So has Bess. I feel they have become a second family to Belinda and me. So I hope you won't worry too much about us. I have faith that everything will work out for us out here. I remind myself often of your favorite quote: "Everything works together for good for those who love the Lord and are called according to His purpose." I believe that everything that has happened so far has been for "His purpose," although I don't understand it all. Keep well, dear Grams, and God bless.

Always,
Your devoted Penny

Chapter 22

That summer was the busiest and happiest Penny could ever recall, different from any other summer of her life. She had never worked so hard nor enjoyed it so much. Her days were filled, and her heart sang with praise to the Creator who had given her a newfound joy in living. Sometimes while on the trail she had felt a hundred years old. Especially after Brad and Thea's deaths, she had been weighted down with a thousand sorrows and uncertainties about the future. Now she could see a new life forming, one she had never dreamed would be hers, one that each day brought more and more into reality.

Owning her own land deepened Penny's appreciation of nature. When she would stop work at noon to eat the picnic lunch Nelldean had packed for her, Penny would sit in quiet contemplation of the rolling hills that surrounded her, listening to the whisper of the gentle wind through her stands of pine and cedar. *Mine,* she would think blissfully — *mine to marvel at and give thanks for; mine to cut for wood to build a house with and to burn in the stove.*

Nate often joined them for their midday meal. From the skinny boy he'd been on the trail, he had grown tall, filled out with the build of a man. All his newly acquired knowledge and skills, after nearly a year of homesteading, he shared liberally with Penny as little by little she developed her land. In spite of his new maturity, Nate still had a boyish grin and an endearing openness. He had a wonderful way with Belinda and had become like a brother to Penny.

And of course, Nelldean had grown even dearer. The bond forged between the older woman and Penny on the trail had become stronger than ever. More and more Penny turned to her for advice and just for the comfort of sharing her innermost thoughts and feelings — particularly about Belinda. What would she do if Belinda was still not speaking when she became old enough to go to school?

Over and over Nelldean would say, "You just have to trust God to work this out, Penny."

Penny knew she was right, but it did not always banish the shadow of fear that Belinda would always be handicapped by the tragedy that had blighted her young life. Sometimes Penny felt it was unfair to burden Nelldean with her own problems, but there was no one else. It wasn't as though she had a husband or Belinda had a father to help shoulder these concerns. She was, after all, alone in the world — and all Belinda had.

Penny tried not to dwell on this. She tried to follow Nelldean's admonition — to live and enjoy each day. For the most part that summer, that's what Penny did.

Another frequent visitor to the homestead that summer was L. C. Boudrey, whose own land was adjacent to Penny's. Once he had found out that Penny was single, his original attraction to her developed rapidly. Because of his uncertain health before then, he had postponed serious courtships. The doctors' dire prediction had been that he had, at best, only a few years to live, and that those would probably be spent in invalidism. Now, with new health and new land, everything seemed possible.

With a freedom he had never felt before, he sensed an optimism about the future and believed he had met the woman who would be his wife: Penny Sayres. Unlike most of the women he knew, she was not married to some miner, for whom she was waiting to return from the gold fields, nor to a soldier at some remote outpost where she and the child could not follow. Neither was she a widow mourning a warrior hero fallen in battle. Every time he saw her his feelings for her grew stronger. He was, however, unsure if she could reciprocate his feelings.

Although she seemed always friendly and glad to see him, grateful for his offers to help with the building and land, their relationship remained merely that of neighbors and friends. L. C. felt it hopeless to expect more. In the first place, he hardly ever had a chance to truly be alone with her. Nelldean, Bess, and Nate were never far away. And of course, there was always Belinda. Although he had not had much experience with children, he found the little girl very appealing and longed to do something to alleviate some of Penny's concern about her. There just never seemed to be an opportunity to discuss it with Penny. By the end of summer L. C. began to wonder if he were on a futile quest.

August merged into the early weeks of September, the most beautiful time of the Oregon year. As the days grew shorter and time out at the homestead grew even more precious, Penny was still making her rounds, selling her line of books, calendars, and almanacs every weekday and spending most of the weekends working on her shelter.

One Saturday in early September, L. C. rode out, hoping to have a little time with her.

As he dismounted, he saw Penny just descending a ladder from the roof of the small shed she was building. He saw her but she had not yet seen him arrive. He tethered his horse under the shade of a giant fir tree and stood watching her as she caught Belinda up in her arms and swung her around. Then putting her cheek against the little girl's round, rosy one, she hugged her. Watching this scene, he caught his breath. He felt his heart move within him. Like a sudden shaft of light passing through his mind, he saw as clearly as if it were projected on a "magic lantern" screen his long-held dream come to life. During the long months of his illness, he had rarely allowed himself the luxury to dream. Life had seemed precariously uncertain. But now, seeing Penny and Belinda, the dream seemed a reality. The hope of happiness, of a wife and a child of his own . . . Suddenly he *knew* Penny was that woman with whom he would want to spend his life, to be his heart's companion, the mother of his children. He had never visualized exactly what she would look like, but seeing Penny holding Belinda, their two heads touching, one golden-red, the other auburn, gleaming in the sunshine, L. C. knew.

He felt a terrible longing to make it all come true. But how could he tell her? Penny had always kept him at arm's length. Whenever the conversation had become the least bit personal, she had turned it by making some amusing remark or by finding something she had to attend to immediately. Always she remained somehow beyond his reach. Was it only coincidence or was it by intent? Did she sense his attraction and wish to discourage it? Yet she always seemed glad to see him when he came. L. C. sighed.

There was so much more to Penny Sayres — resourceful, courageous, strong. What a woman she was! But on the other side of the coin of his admiration was the question, Was she too independent to need a man — even a man who would love her for those very qualities and respect that very independence?

His thoughts came to an abrupt end when she suddenly looked over Belinda's head and saw him. After setting the little girl back on the ground, she waved.

"Come see how much we've done. Nelldean says we should have a roof-raising celebration when we've nailed the last shingle."

L. C. walked over to where she stood. He looked up at the small building, now nearly completed, and admired it with her.

"Won't you stay and have some lemonade and gingerbread with us?" Penny invited. "Bess brought some out earlier, then stole away my helper," she laughed gaily. "She captured Nelldean to help her at the church this afternoon. They're having a blackberry festival this weekend. Like blackberry pie? There'll be a whole mountain of them at the social."

Penny went down to the stream that ran close by and brought back the tin container of lemonade they had placed securely between rocks in the water to chill. She poured them each a tumbler full, then opened the basket in which a loaf of gingerbread was wrapped in a blue and white checkered napkin, and cut slices for the three of them.

After they ate, Belinda took the rag doll Nelldean had made her on the trail, the one she was rarely without, over to a shady spot at a little distance from where Penny and L. C. sat. She placed the doll against the trunk of the tree and began making a playhouse from twigs and leaves.

A quiet peace settled over the little valley. L. C. glanced at Penny. She had never looked prettier. Golden freckles sprinkled across the bridge of her nose and on her lightly tanned skin. The afternoon sun sent small sparkles of light through her hair, which was twisted up carelessly into a knot on top of her head. He found himself longing to touch the stray curls that spiraled onto her neck. Would this be a good time to tell her that he had fallen in love with her?

Even as he asked himself this he saw the expression on Penny's face change. She was watching Belinda picking wildflowers and fashioning them into little bouquets. The tenderness on Penny's face as she gazed at the little girl brought a sharp question to L. C.'s mind. Uncertainty took the place of decision. Was there room in Penny's heart for anyone else? As he was asking himself this, she sighed and when she turned to him her eyes were moist.

"I wish I knew what to do. If only I could help her some way — to find her voice again."

L. C. recognized this as a rare opportunity. He did not want to ruin this moment of intimacy, nor did he want to overstep the bounds of the confidence she was tentatively extending.

She proceeded to tell him about their journey west, what they had been through, and how Belinda had stopped speaking after Thea's death. "That's why the decision to stay here was so hard for me to make, even though I really had nothing to go back to. . . ." Her voice trailed off. "I've wondered if I shouldn't have made the effort to go back for *her* sake. Maybe there's a doctor back east who could do something —"

"But from what you told me it's not medical —," L. C. ventured. "I mean, there's no physical cause for her not to talk. She talked before, didn't she —"

"Oh, yes. Well, not always understandable, except for a few words like Mama, Dada, Penny, milk cow — that sort of thing. But she babbled constantly as though she knew what she was saying. And she certainly isn't . . . well, there's nothing wrong with her mind. She's smart as she can be. Nelldean says in time she'll talk."

"Nelldean's right, you know. I know men who were in the war who went dumb from shock. Maybe that's what's happened to Belinda. From all that happened to your wagon train . . . I mean, how can a small child understand all those terrible things? Maybe the only way she could handle it was to retreat back into babyhood — into not having to put it all into words."

The little frown that had puckered Penny's brows together over her troubled eyes cleared. "Yes. You're probably right. And Nelldean is too. I just need to have more faith. She keeps reminding me of Mark 7:37: 'He makes both the deaf to hear and the mute to speak.' I just hope Belinda's healing isn't dependent on my believing it will happen."

Penny looked so sad that L. C. longed to

reach out, take her in his arms, and comfort her. Much as he longed to, he knew it was not the time. All uncertainty about his own feelings vanished. Everything within him yearned to comfort and assure her that she need not worry or go through this *alone.* He was sure now that he wanted to take care of her *and* Belinda, to make things secure and safe for her whatever happened. But he realized it was too soon. He had to make her trust him first. . . .

Just then Nate Hardison came thundering down the hill on his horse and the moment of intimacy ended. Nate was one of Belinda's favorite people, and as he jumped off his horse, she ran toward him. He lifted her up into his saddle, where she smiled happily.

"How's it goin'?" Nate asked Penny, cheerfully leading the horse and little rider over to where she and L. C. were sitting.

The conversation became general then, of tree felling, timber, boards, caulking, fence posts, and rafters.

Then Nate grinned and said, "Trout are plentiful in the pond upstream. How about goin' fishin'? Catch us a few browns we can have for supper? Gramma and Bess can fry us up a batch and some good ol' cornpone with it!"

From the look on Belinda's face, there was

no doubt she understood what Nate had proposed. She began to clap her chubby hands
together. Nate got her down from the horse,
saying, "Come on, Belinda, let's cut us some
birch poles for rods. I'll get one for you,
Penny," he called over his shoulder as, hand
in hand, he and Belinda headed for the edge
of the stream.

L. C. got to his feet and said good-bye. As
he mounted his horse, he saw Penny hurrying
off in the direction Nate and Belinda had
gone. He rode back to town wishing he'd
been invited to go fishing too.

Chapter 23

One September evening not long after L.C.'s visit, Penny was on her way home from a long day of selling, and her thoughts turned to Belinda. Would she ever speak again? She seemed happy enough: no tantrums, no moping, no visible signs that might be attributed to the tragic happenings of her young life other than her refusal to speak. Every characteristic was that of a normal three-year-old child. Penny knew there was nothing wrong with her mind. Belinda reacted to everything about her, her eyes held intelligence and responsiveness. When Penny played word games or acted out stories with Belinda's dolls or played tricks that might make her react verbally, Belinda enjoyed it all immensely, laughing out loud, clapping her hands, playing the games. But still she didn't talk.

Penny sighed. She couldn't be with the little girl every minute. When Penny was out working on her route, Belinda seemed quite content to stay with Nelldean and Bess, who adored the little girl. Penny knew she was lucky to have them taking care of Belinda while she earned money to support them. But maybe — suddenly, a thought struck her. Just *maybe* — that was *it!* With the two grandmas catering to Belinda's every whim, anticipating her needs so that she never even needed to ask for anything, there was no necessity for the child to talk!

Penny put the buggy in the lean-to, unharnessed Jebo, slipped a feed bag over his nose, and went into the house, still deep in thought. She found Nelldean in the kitchen, sewing one of her sunbonnets. Since coming to Oregon City, Nelldean had got a thriving little business going making sunbonnets. Mr. Miller carried all she could supply and paid her a nice sum for each one.

She greeted Penny cheerfully. "Have a good day? Belinda's already in bed. She fell asleep whilst I was rockin' her. I kept your supper hot on the back of the stove. Sit yourself down and I'll serve you."

Penny pulled out one of the chairs and sat down gratefully.

"You're too good to me, Nelldean, you spoil me. Spoil us both. Me and Belinda!"

"Nuthin' of the kind!" Nelldean retorted. "I like doin' for folks. And you and Belinda's like my own. People what's been through what we've been together get like this —," she held up crossed fingers and quoted, "Ecclesiastes 4:9 — 'a threefold cord is not easily broken.' That's us: you, me, and Belinda."

"What about Nate? Doesn't he fit in with us too?" Penny teased.

Nelldean put Penny's plate of steaming pot roast, potatoes, and cabbage in front of her, then sat down again across from her at the table.

"Well, I've got some news to tell you," Nelldean said picking up her sewing again and frowning at the ruffle she was slipstitching around the brim. "Nate was by here earlier; got me to sew on a button or two — all slicked up he was." She paused significantly. "Goin' courtin'." She glanced at Penny for her reaction.

"Courting? Nate?" Penny's fork halted halfway to her mouth.

"Yessiree. Zeire McCall, no less. Reverend McCall's daughter. Seems he met her at the blackberry social and, well —"

"Do you think — I mean is it serious?"

Nelldean chuckled, "Seems so. Leastways, he said he cain't wait till spring to frame up his house. Suddenly, sleeping in the barn he put up don't seem to suit."

"Nate thinking about getting married!" Penny shook her head.

"Well, maybe not right away, but —," she

paused for a few seconds before going on. "It's the best thing that could have happened. I'm happy about it. She's a real sweet girl."

"But what about you, Nelldean? You came out here to be with Nate, to live with him on the homestead."

"Oh, honey, I didn't 'spect Nate to stay a bachelor forever. Nor do I 'spect to live forever. Nate's got a good head on his shoulders, smart and responsible for his age. He's got a nice homestead started, planted an orchard. It could've gone another way entirely — what with all the temptations out here for a single man. And you know what Scripture says: 'It's not good for man to be alone.' "

Nelldean stopped and looked over her spectacles at Penny for a long moment, as if expecting her to say something.

Penny suppressed a smile. Nelldean was always hinting that L. C.'s intentions toward her were serious, but Penny dismissed them. She had already taken on as much as she could handle. Marriage certainly wasn't in her plans. Not now, not yet. Maybe not ever. Her first responsibility was toward Belinda. Until Belinda was completely recovered, nothing else was important. But now she was concerned about Nelldean. With Nate making plans of his own, what about his grandmother?

Impulsively Penny reached across the table and squeezed Nelldean's arm.

"Well, you'll always have a home with us, Nelldean. Next spring my house will be going up, and we'll all live there as snug as can be."

Nelldean's eyes misted, and she had to remove her glasses and wipe them before replying. "Don't forget about yourself, Penny. You've got a life of your own too."

"I won't, and I know I do, Nelldean. But right now Belinda is more important. I've been thinking a lot about how to get her talking. I think I need to spend more time alone with her. And this is what I'm thinking. The weather is still nice; the mornings are cool, but the days are mostly sunny and warm." As she spoke a plan began to form in Penny's mind. "I want to take Belinda on a little camping trip this next weekend. She'd love it. Remember how I used to put her on the saddle with me on the trail? We'll take blanket rolls, gear, and enough food for a couple of days. We'll fish and hike, and maybe I can get her talking. If we're out there alone together, maybe she'll have to start asking for things — speaking!"

Nelldean looked thoughtful. "Yes, that just might do it. At least you can give it a try. She's a good little camper. It just might work, Penny."

With Nelldean's encouragement Penny went ahead with her plans. Although Bess was more constrained in her support of the idea.

"I don't know, Penny," she said doubtfully. "You folks ain't been out here long enough to know, but Oregon weather, especially this time of year, is mighty changeable. It might turn real quick."

Bess tended to be a worrywart, and Penny blandly dismissed her warning. "We'll take plenty of blankets and warm clothes," Penny assured her and went on packing.

When told about their adventure, Belinda seemed delighted and began to help getting ready, bringing her doll and a favorite raggedy blanket to be included in the packing. Penny filled the saddle bags with enough supplies for a couple of days. Then she placed Belinda astride the saddle, then mounted herself. With admonitions from Nelldean and Bess to be careful, they set out.

The morning was glorious. The sun touched the leaves on the trees, turning them to brilliant yellow and russet all along the roadway out of town.

"We're going to have such a wonderful time, honey," Penny told her. "We'll go out to the homestead first, then we can climb up into the hills, find a stream to fish in, explore the other side of their property, pick wild-flowers —" She felt the child's arms tighten around her waist. "You'll like that, won't you, honey? They're so many fun things we can do. Then we can make a camp, build a fire to cook our meals. Nothing more delicious than fresh-caught fish fried along with potatoes sliced with wild onions found along banks of the creek, is there, Belinda? And tonight we'll sleep under the stars in our blanket rolls like a couple of cowboys!" She heard Belinda's lilting little laugh and knew the child was understanding and enjoying the prospect. *Please God,* Penny prayed. *Maybe, just maybe, when we're alone, Belinda might talk again.*

That first day was wonderful. The fresh air revived Penny, who had worked especially hard all week so as not to feel guilty by missing two good working days. The further they went, the more reassured Penny felt that she had not made a mistake deciding to stay in Oregon. They would be happy on their homestead; she would create a real home for Belinda and herself. As they rode along she could picture herself planting fruit trees on the sloping hills, putting in a large vegetable garden, perhaps, and having some milk cows and goats. More and more she could envision the life they could have here. If only Belinda would recover her speech. . . .

When the shadows on the hills began to shroud the sun, Penny decided to camp for the night. There was a rippling stream and large trees with low sweeping branches under which they could be safely sheltered and spread their blanket rolls. She set Belinda busily gathering small twigs and branches to get a fire started while she got out a frying pan and the slices of bacon Nelldean had wrapped in cheesecloth in their food pack. She got a can full of water from the stream and made a pot of the best coffee she had ever tasted from the sweet clear water. They ate hungrily after the day out in the open, and afterward Belinda looked drowsy. As the moon began to rise over the tips of the pines, Penny gathered Belinda close in her arms and sang her to sleep with an old hymn she had learned in childhood: "How gracious you have been to me, O Lord, how bountiful in thy gifts." Her voice rose sweetly upward into the night air.

They awakened at first light. They rolled up their blankets and washed their faces in the stream. Penny stirred up the fire, made coffee, then they ate the potatoes they had buried in the embers the night before to roast.

It was a splendid cloudless blue day. Invigorated, Penny decided to climb higher up into the hills. The sun was gilding everything, the light frost melting away in glistening diamonds, the aspen trees along the path quivered in the crisp breeze. As they wound up through the wooded hillside they could look down into the valley and see the colorful patches of red maples, the golden willows, and the silver ribbon of the stream bending through. The way became steeper and every so often Penny turned the horse aside to let her rest and nibble at the grasses. It was a different kind of day than their first one but just as enjoyable, and the scenery at this level was even more spectacular. Penny was filled with awe at the wonder of God's creation.

At this elevation, however, the day seemed to darken sooner and she began looking for a place to camp for the night. They reached a clearing surrounded by magnificent cedars. The fallen needles had made a soft mattress on which they could lay their bedrolls to sleep in comfort from the wind that was growing quite chilly. Penny made a fire and they cooked the trout they had caught the day before. With a dessert of dried apples and shortbread brought from home they had a fine supper. By the time they finished it was already dark, so they tucked in for the night on a mattress of pine needles under a lean-to of sweeping cedar boughs. Belinda went straight to sleep, but Penny, though pleasantly tired from the exertion of the day, lay awake listening to the wind sigh through the branches, and she prided herself on her accomplishments. Who, knowing her back in Dunwoodie, would ever have thought that she could take a child and set out alone on a three day camping trip? It even amazed *her*. As she finally drifted off to sleep, she felt proud of her newly developed independence and capability.

But the minute she opened her eyes, the proverbial prediction popped into her mind: "Pride goeth before a fall." After waking, she lay there for a moment listening. She heard nothing but silence. Not a whisper of wind, nor the stirring of a tree limb. Slowly it came to her. It had snowed during the night and a white blanket of heavy snow covered everything for as far as she could see. Moving carefully she slid out from under her bedroll. As she did her head hit a low branch of the tree under which they were sleeping, and a shower of snow landed on her! After brushing the snow out of her eyes, Penny marveled at the beauty of it all.

Then slowly she realized their predicament. This must be one of those "freak" snowstorms Penny had heard about. After her first awe at its beauty, Penny decided they had better try to get back to town in case there was more snow in the offing. However, this proved more difficult than she anticipated. The snow was soft and deep, and the trail they had taken coming up was completely obliterated.

The sky, heavy with gray clouds, looked as if there might be more snow on the way. Penny debated whether to try to make it back to the homestead or to remain where she was. Riding a horse with a child clinging to your waist down a steep grade in a snowstorm would be no easy task. But there seemed nothing else to do but try. After a hasty breakfast, Penny packed their bedrolls and saddle bags onto the patient Jebo; then she lifted Belinda up and mounted herself. Slowly, they started back down the hill they had climbed so confidently the day before. Jebo valiantly did his best, but he kept stumbling. Penny held her breath, afraid that she would be pitched off with Belinda and tossed down over the unseen cliffs. Holding tight to the reins, they inched down the hazardous mountainside.

Every so often a tree limb, heavy with snow, would suddenly shift in the wind and dump its load down their backs. At last they managed to get down the mountain and reach a clearing. Penny got off and walked over to the edge where she could see down into the valley. There, very faintly, she made out the outline of the slanted roof of her homestead shelter.

"Oh, thank God!" she breathed a sigh. "It's all right, Belinda, we're almost home!" she called gaily to the child, who was so bundled up that only her little cherry nose peeked out from the scarf and cap.

Torturously they made the last hazardous few miles down. But afternoon shadows were lengthening rapidly and there was definitely a scent of snow in the cold air. Penny led Jebo into the lean-to beside their shack and unloaded him. She took off the saddle and bags, threw a blanket over him, then carried Belinda into the small cabin.

Keeping up cheerful chatter, Penny was grateful that Nate had installed a small stove in addition to her bunk and a couple of chairs. All this was done mainly to fulfill the homestead requirements of building a livable shelter on the property within a year of the claim. At least they had a few supplies here and enough firewood to keep them warm for a day or two.

Contrite at having put themselves in this risky situation, Penny blamed herself. She had been foolhardy and over-confident to take a small child on a camping expedition without making provisions for an emergency. She also knew that by now Nelldean and Bess would be concerned about them, and she felt bad to have caused them any worry.

If the snow continued — if it became one of those blizzards she'd heard about — they could be marooned for days. At the worst, they could freeze to death, if their wood burned out, or if their food gave out, they could starve before anyone could come to rescue them. Before her fears got out of control, Penny recalled Grams' often-used comment: "Don't borrow trouble" or better still "Sufficient for the day. . . ."

Give us this day our daily bread. She *had* that, Penny reminded herself as she unwrapped half a loaf, some cheese. *Manna.* She smiled to herself. God had provided for the complaining Israelites even if they had got themselves as lost in the desert as she had been in the foothills. "Trust in the Lord, and he will provide *all* your needs." *Why do we have to be brought to our knees before we really rely on his gracious providence? "O ye of little faith!" I'm full of Scripture quotations today,* Penny chided herself in amusement. Nevertheless, she found them comforting.

She got a fire going in the little stove and put some bacon in a skillet. Scooping some snow from outside the door into two buckets, she set one aside to melt so that she could take it out for Jebo to drink. The other bucket she set in front of the stove so that she could later pour it into a kettle to boil for coffee. On the shelf she found a jug of molasses, some canned milk, and a tin of beans. "Enough for a fine supper!" Penny exclaimed triumphantly to Belinda. Their meal turned out to be delicious and satisfying along with fried bacon and what was left of the loaf of bread. Afterward, when Belinda's eyes began to droop sleepily, Penny wrapped her up snugly on the low bunk bed, and Belinda was asleep in a minute.

Sipping a second cup of coffee, Penny went to the window. All she could see was an endless carpet of snow. Involuntarily she shivered. Tomorrow she might have to turn Jebo loose to find the trail back to town. That way someone would surely come looking for them.

"And I'll be ready to eat some humble pie," Penny said to herself as she unrolled her blanket and crawled in beside Belinda. She lay there watching the fire until she too fell asleep.

To her amazement she slept dreamlessly. When she first awakened she could not remember right away where she was. She raised her head and looked around the small cabin. Gradually things came back to mind. Then she saw Belinda standing on a stool looking out the cabin window. "Morning, honey," Penny called to her as she got out of the bunk. Belinda turned to look at her, then pointed her chubby little finger and said over and over, "Snow, pitty snow!"

They were the very words Penny had repeated to her over and over the day before trying to keep her from being afraid as they made their precarious way down the mountainside!

The shock of hearing Belinda's voice momentarily immobilized Penny. Belinda had *spoken.* Actually spoken *out loud!* She *could* speak! She *was* speaking! O dear God, thank you! Penny almost choked on her own rush of thanksgiving. She jumped up and ran over to the little girl. Laughing and crying for joy, Penny hugged Belinda.

"Yes, darling, I see it, I *see* it! Pretty snow." Holding her, Penny looked out to where the new snow was falling, drifting like big goose feathers out of a milky gray sky.

All that long day Penny talked to Belinda and Belinda chattered back. She repeated whatever Penny said. Penny would point to articles of clothing, every item in the cabin, to her eyes, to her nose, to her mouth, her ears, her hair and teeth. The little girl would say it again and again. In between Penny could not resist hugging and kissing her, praising her, which made the little girl laugh merrily.

They invented games, and Penny began to tell her stories. "Once upon a time —," Penny would start, and Belinda would reply, "Once pont da time."

In her joy over Belinda's recovery, Penny alternated between laughter and tears, almost forgetting their predicament. Early in the afternoon she noticed that the pale sun was trying to penetrate the clouds and the listless snow had ceased to fall.

Later still, when she again went to the window to check the weather, Penny saw a figure on horseback coming through the drifts toward the cabin. Pressing her face against the glass, she peered out trying to see better. Had Nelldean sent Nate? But the rider looked taller, broader of shoulder than Nelldean's grandson. His sheepskin collar was turned high, his broad-brimmed slouch hat low so that his face was obscured. But there was something vaguely familiar about him. Penny rushed to the door, flung it open just as the rider dismounted. To her total astonishment she saw it was L. C. Boudrey.

"Oh, I'm *so* glad to see you," she called to him in a voice warm with gratitude. "How did you find us?"

He explained that he had seen them start out on their camping trip from his office window that Friday. Later, he had run into Nell on the street and, after judicious questioning, learned where they were going. Then with the snowstorm, he became worried about them. Since the homestead claim wasn't far from his ranch, he set out to find them — to rescue them, if need be.

"Come in, come in," Penny invited him, taking hold of his arm and bringing him inside.

"You're all right then?" he asked, brushing the snow from the shoulder of his jacket before stepping over the threshold. "And the little one, too?"

"Better than all right. Something wonderful has happened. It's Belinda." Penny ran over to the little girl.

"She's talking?" L. C. asked.

"*Talking?* She hasn't stopped since she first saw the snow early this morning." She picked her up in her arms and coached, "Say hello, darling."

"Heddo dawding!" the child repeated. Penny and L. C. looked at each other, then burst out laughing. Belinda, pleased that she had said something to make the grownups laugh, repeated it over and over — "Heddo, dawding, heddo dawding . . ." — interspersed with giggles, until they were all in a hilarious mood.

"It's Mr. Boudrey, Belinda. Boudrey," Penny prompted.

"Bouey! Bouey!" Belinda repeated, laughing.

Penny gave her a squeeze. "Oh, you're a little minx, aren't you! Now say hello properly to Mr. Boudrey."

Belinda stuck her chubby finger in her mouth, then in a very loud voice said, "Bouey! Bouey!" to another round of laughter.

"I can't tell you how happy I am. It's an answer to prayer. A great many prayers. I feel everything's going to be all right now." Penny smiled and poured L. C. a cup of coffee.

"Well, we better start back soon. More snow's predicted, and I'd feel better if we were safely on our way before that happens. Mrs. Hardison and Mrs. Fulton were mighty worried. And, of course, so was I."

"It was so good of you to come all this way out here to find us."

Within the hour, L. C. had packed up, and then Penny and Belinda, bundled up again, mounted. They followed the trail made by L. C. earlier. It would be a slow trip but a safe one.

As they headed out, Penny said, "I can't thank you enough for coming. I'm not sure how long my firewood and food would have lasted."

"No thanks necessary. It gave me a chance

I always dreamed about when I was a little boy."

"What was that?"

"Being a knight on horseback coming to rescue a damsel in distress. In this case, *two* damsels," he laughed, nodding toward Belinda.

"Well, it's nice to know dreams sometimes come true," Penny replied.

"Not all do, but we can keep hoping." L. C.'s eyes held amusement and something else Penny could not quite discern. "I must say, though, it was a pretty *capable* damsel I found. You could have done quite nicely on your own for another few days, I'm sure."

Chapter 24

During Penny's second spring in Oregon, two things happened that brought her to a decision. One was the celebration of Belinda's third birthday, and the other was the announcement of Nate Hardison's intention to wed the preacher's daughter, Zeire McCall. Ever since Belinda had recovered her ability to speak, she had filled the house with childish chatter, endless questions, and merry laughter. Nelldean and Bess were overjoyed at Belinda's recovery, and the child was even more the center of attention.

Penny now had enough money saved to hire a carpenter to build on to the original shed and construct a small house on the homestead where she and Belinda could live and where, when Nate got married, Nelldean would join them.

The night of the engagement party, Penny was late going to bed. She had insisted that Nelldean and Bess, both exhausted by all the preparations, go to bed and let her clean up the kitchen. After all was finished, she pulled a rocking chair up to the window and sat for a long time looking out at a beautiful moonlit night. A night for romance and lovers. She smiled, thinking of the looks exchanged between Nate and Zeire as they had accepted the congratulations and well wishes of friends. Sipping a cup of tea, Penny let her mind wander back to some of her own romantic dreams. Dreams that seemed to have been those of a girl she now hardly knew.

What had happened to her? All sorts of things had made her grow up and become a realist, a person who did not allow herself the luxury of dreams.

Enough! she told herself and quickly got up, put away her cup, banked the fire in the stove, and tiptoed into the small bedroom she shared with Belinda. Looking down at the sleeping child, Penny decided it was time to adopt her legally, time that they became a *real* family. She would need legal advice about how to go about the adoption. L. C. was the logical person to consult.

One day soon afterward she ran into him on Main Street as she was coming from the post office. As always, L. C. seemed happy to see her. Although after "rescuing" them he had been a frequent visitor to the Fulton house, lately he hadn't come quite as often. Penny wondered why. Nelldean had been more to the point when Penny remarked on it one day.

"Why not, indeed?" Nelldean said in a slightly indignant tone of voice. "The man's not a fool. Why should he keep minin' where there's no gold? He don't get much encouragement," she said with a sniff.

"Why, what do you mean? We're always glad to see him. Belinda always rushes to greet him. And I always enjoy his visits."

"Humph. Not so anyone could notice," retorted Nelldean with a little toss of her head.

"Why, Nelldean, how can you say that! I'll always be grateful to him for coming to dig us out that day and being so kind to Belinda."

"I don't think it's *gratitude* he's lookin' for." She gave Penny another look, seemed about to say something, then pressed her lips together. She gave the cake batter she was beating a few hard licks, tapping the wooden spoon on the edge of the stoneware bowl, then said, "Mebbe he's findin' a warmer welcome elsewhere in town. A fine lookin' gentleman like him's bound to catch many a lady's eye and be ushered happily into any parlor in this town."

The conversation might have gone further, but Bess came in. Penny was just as glad. She had other things on her mind at the moment.

She was, however, recalling that exchange with Nelldean as she saw L. C. approaching.

"Good day, Miss Sayres." He tipped his hat

and stopped. "How nice to see you."

"And what a coincidence seeing *you,* Mr. Boudrey."

"How's that?"

"Well, I was just thinking about you and —"

"You *were?*"

His eyes lighted up so eagerly she was almost embarrassed to tell him why she had been thinking of him.

"Yes, sometime soon, I want to consult you on a legal matter. I shall come to your office and discuss it, if I may?"

The light seemed to fade from his eyes, but he inclined his head and his voice took on the professionally correct tone.

"Any way I may be of help, I would be most happy to do so."

"I shall make an appointment then in a few days."

"Any time, Miss Sayres, it would be my pleasure." He paused slightly, then asked, "And how is Belinda?"

"Oh, fine! Chattering like a magpie all the time now." Penny was about to say something like, "Why don't you come see for yourself?" but checked herself. Remembering what Nelldean had suggested might be his reason for staying away, Penny felt reluctant to indicate that he had been missed or to issue a particular invitation for him to call.

They stood there for a moment, neither making a move to leave. Then L. C. tipped his hat again, bowed, and continued on down the street.

Penny looked after him, puzzled, then with a slight shrug walked home. Among the mail was a letter from Grams. She was anxious to read it since it had been at least three months since she'd heard from her grandmother.

The letter contained much heartfelt relief, happiness, and "Praise the Lords" over the news of Belinda's newfound speech. Grams also enclosed a clipping from the Dunwoodie newspaper, to which she attached an explanatory note: "I thought you'd be especially interested in seeing this item that ran in our *Independent* last week."

"EXPERIENCED GUIDE TO LEAD GROUP TO CALIFORNIA" was the headline. Penny's eyes widened as she read the article:

Jeremiah Bradshaw, lay evangelist and seasoned traveler, successful traveler of the famous Oregon Trail, will speak tonight at the Town Hall and recruit emigrants to make the trip under his guidance to the rich western territory of California. Mr. Bradshaw's lecture will include pictures of the fruitful orchards, orange groves, and gold fields —

Penny finished reading the rest of the piece with growing disbelief. How could Jeremiah pass himself off as an "experienced guide" when he hadn't even completed the trip? And where was poor Emily in all this? Were they still together? Was she still alive even?

Penny tore up the clipping in disgust. She pitied the poor people who took him at his word and invested in expensive equipment to undertake the journey under his command. She could hardly suppress a shudder remembering her last encounter with Jeremiah. Well, thankfully, that was all in the past. At least *she* would never have to see him or have any contact with him ever again.

The following Friday afternoon, after completing her sales for the week, Penny went to L. C.'s law office. From his window he had seen her coming down the boardwalk. With admiration he watched her cross the street. How attractive she was! The proud lift of her head, the erect, purposeful walk. He went to the door and stood there, waiting for her knock.

"Come in, Miss Sayres."

"You act as though you were expecting me, Mr. Boudrey."

"You did mention that you might be needing some legal assistance, so I am not completely surprised. Won't you have a seat? Now, what can I do for you?"

"I want to fill out papers or whatever is necessary to adopt Belinda," Penny said as she settled herself in the chair L. C. drew up for her to the side of his roll-top desk.

"Since she has no other living relatives and you are her blood kin, that should be easily arranged."

"I want her to be co-owner of the homestead property or at least the beneficiary of my estate — I mean, whatever I accumulate in my lifetime — at my death."

"We can draw up that kind of agreement as well. They would be two separate documents, of course."

"I know nothing of legal matters. Will you take care of this for me then, Mr. Boudrey?"

"Of course, but may I ask a favor of you, Miss Sayres?"

"Certainly."

"Since we have known each other over a period of time now, could you bring yourself to call me by my first name?"

Penny looked surprised and rather amused. He was so serious.

"Why, yes. That is, except —"

"Except?"

"There's something I've wanted to ask you

for a long time," she said.

"Ask away."

"Well, it's a rather personal question, and I've often been told I am too blunt —"

"Not for me. I like frankness. I encourage it in my clients." He smiled.

"You're sure?"

"Indeed. What would you like to know?"

"I'm curious, how can I call you by your first name when all I know is the initials L. C.?"

Something curious flickered in his eyes regarding her. "My friends call me Lot," he answered.

"*Lot?* You mean like in the Bible?" Penny exclaimed. Then, thinking her amusement might seem like ridicule, she rushed on: "*Really?* It seems a rather strange name to give a child. Lot was *not* the most heroic of characters in the Bible. One would think that if parents were going to choose a biblical name, another selection, like Abraham or David, might —," she halted, her hand went to her mouth in embarrassment. "Not that I mean to criticize your parents for choosing it, but —" Again she stopped. "It *is* a little unusual, isn't it?"

He laughed. "I wasn't there at the time I was named, so I really had no say in the choice. By the way, is *Penny* your real name?"

"I asked you first," she parried.

"All right. But I warn you, I've only let a few people in on this deep, dark secret. Actually my name is Lancelot. My mother was a devotee of Tennyson and was reading *The Idylls of the King* when she was expecting me. She was entranced by the whole round table legend and named her only son after the shining knight." He smiled. "Unhappily, the famous knight turned out not be quite so chivalrous as she had supposed. I was born and named before she got to the end of the story. And then it was too late. As I was growing up, my family and friends all called me Lance. But when I came out west and hung up my shingle as a lawyer, I just used my initials. Actually, no one else has ever asked me about it before now." He paused. Penny looked as if she were having trouble keeping a straight face. "I know it's pretty unlikely," he added. "I warned you."

"Well, it's not only funny. It's a kind of co-incidence —"

"How so? You mean both our mothers gave us 'storybook names'? That is, if I'm assuming correctly that *your real* name, of course, is Penelope. Right? After the noble, patient, faithful wife of Ulysses?"

Penny shook her head. "No. Penny is a nickname from when I was little — and people used to tease me about the color of my hair." She drew out a strand from under her bonnet brim, "Coppery like a penny. Somehow it stuck. Probably because they were all disappointed."

"Disappointed?"

"You see, I was named for a distant relative, an elderly cousin, who everyone hoped would be flattered and leave me a fortune when she died. I think she must have been very wealthy, or why else would a family give a child such a name, unless they had hopes of a great inheritance?" Penny laughed. "As it turned out, she wasn't all that rich and in her will left most of her money to a number of cats she adored. Would you believe this particular relative was considered a little eccentric by the rest of the family — *bookish* —" Mischief danced in her eyes. "That she was considered very suspect . . . a person who read a lot . . . poetry especially."

"But you still haven't told me what your name really is. What is the coincidence you mentioned?"

"Well, if you want to know the truth, my real name is . . . Guinevere!"

"What? Guinevere? Truly?"

"Yes, really and truly!"

He threw his head back, roaring with laughter. When he finally got control of himself, he demanded, "You mean . . . ?"

"*Yes* — her favorite poetic characters were —," and they both finished together, "King Arthur and the knights of the round table!"

"So now we've found out all sorts of things about each other. Any more hidden secrets, any other family skeletons in your closet you want to confess?" he asked teasingly.

"No, I don't think so. But there is one request I'd like to make."

"Granted," he said promptly. "You don't need to ask. Whatever you want, it's yours."

"That's an unwise statement. Especially for a lawyer," she admonished playfully.

"Go ahead. Ask away. If it's in my power to give it, I will."

"Oh, it is," Penny told him. "You said most of your friends call you Lot?"

He nodded.

"But I'm sure your mother didn't. What did she call you?"

His eyes softened and he answered, "Lance."

"Yes, that's much better. I like that. You asked me to call you by your given name. She must have loved that name. May I call you Lance too?"

"I'd be very pleased if you did — Penny." He said her name almost tenderly.

"Good. Then it's settled." Penny rose. "I

must go." She went to the door and stood there for a moment putting on her gloves. "If you don't have other plans, Nelldean told me to be sure to ask if you'd come to supper this evening?"

On his feet, Lance smiled. "Delighted. Do thank her for the gracious invitation."

"I shall." Penny's cheeks dimpled. "See you about six then?"

"With pleasure." He walked with her to the door. There she hesitated a second, then looked up at him with mischief in her eyes. "So what does the C stand for?"

"The C?" He frowned. "Oh, the C! Calhoun! My mother was a southern sympathizer," he laughed.

"Another family skeleton!" She joined in his laughter. "Well, good-bye for now."

His eyes followed her as she went down the steps and over to her small buggy. What a magnificent woman. How lucky any man would be. . . .

As Penny picked up the reins and flicked them lightly across Jebo's back, she glanced back to where L. C. Boudrey — Lance — was still standing in his office door. She waved and he waved back. As she drove off, she realized she was looking forward to the evening more than she had anything for a very long time.

★ ★ ★

A week later Lance stopped by the house. Nelldean answered the door, then went to call Penny, who was reading to Belinda. Diplomatically, Nelldean coaxed Belinda, with a bribe of cookies, to stay with her while Penny went into the tiny parlor where Mr. Boudrey was waiting.

"I hope I'm not calling at an inconvenient time, but there were a few questions I wanted to ask before I file your adoption request papers. I also wanted to make some suggestions that might facilitate a speedy resolution."

"Yes, of course. You don't foresee any serious problems, do you?"

"No, not really. There's one thing that, as your lawyer, I may want to advise you to change on the application."

"Oh? Well, of course, I should consider very carefully any advice you have. I want this done as speedily as possible. What would you have me change?"

He took a sheaf of papers from his thin leather briefcase and held the top one out for Penny. "See right here, where it says Guinevere Sayres: spinster — I'd like that changed."

"Changed? You mean you'd rather I use Penny, so it won't sound so — so fanciful — to some judge who will be making the decision?"

"No, Guinevere is fine as it is. It's the *spinster* I'd like to see changed."

Penny turned wide puzzled eyes on him.

"Penny, I want that changed to *married*. . . . I want — I am asking you to marry me. . . . You look so surprised. You never guessed?"

She shook her head.

"Didn't you realize I'm in love with you?"

"Perhaps you *think* you are."

"I'm not exactly a boy to confuse attraction or infatuation with love, Miss Sayres."

"And I, Mr. Boudrey, am no longer a girl — full of foolish dreams of romance and knights riding to the rescue on white chargers."

"Ah, but then. . . ." He smiled, rubbed his chin with one hand, his eyes filling with amusement. "You can never tell. And love means different things to different people —"

"Mostly different to men than to women."

"Maybe. But let me at least say this. That very first day we met, I *knew* — though I didn't know *how* I knew. And I didn't know exactly how it would all turn out, knowing life is not always a poem or a story with a happy ending. Still, I knew that somehow we were meant to be together. And I still do," Lance said softly. "Lancelot and Guinevere! Imagine! That is no ordinary coincidence. The more I think about it, the more convinced I am that our meeting was destined. It *had* to be . . . it was so ridiculous, so preordained . . . I'm *never* home at that time of day . . . usually . . . and then you came and —"

"You're too imaginative. Much too imaginative for a *lawyer!*" Penny chided him, trying to be severe. "Lawyers are supposed to be all facts, every *t* crossed, every *i* dotted. Not irrational or fanciful like the rest of us."

"Lawyers are human too, Penny. Lawyers *in love* are maybe even more capable of poetry and romance, because it's unusual for them. I *know* I love you, and I want you to marry me. It's not an impulse. I've been thinking of it for a long time. In fact, lately I've thought of nothing else. Will you, Penny? Will you marry me, change that word *spinster* and become my wife?"

Penny was quiet for what seemed a very long time. But he waited. As a lawyer, he knew about timing: he knew how to wait for a jury to absorb testimony and how to watch for a person to reveal something under cross-examination. He knew how to make a summary statement and assess its impact on a courtroom, how to debate the options and deliberate the verdict. So he waited, all the while longing to gently brush back the coppery hair, touch the smooth curve of her cheek, kiss the sweet, vulnerable mouth. He waited. . . .

The silence lengthened between them, then Penny spoke slowly, "I've been so busy, so preoccupied, I haven't allowed myself to dream of love. I do respect you, and I'm touched and honored that you have asked me to marry you. I think I need time —"

"I understand that. I don't mean to rush or pressure. As for this —," Lance gently withdrew the papers he had handed her "— you can go ahead with this as it is. I used it as a device to propose." He gave a rueful smile. "Lawyer's trick. Forgive me."

Penny studied him for a long minute. From the very first day, she had been impressed by him. As she got to know him she realized he had the all the qualities she had always admired in a man but had never found in one man before. He had overcome his own challenges well, regained his health, and established a law practice and reputation in a new community. He was outstanding in every way: of obvious strength of character, with an optimistic faith, intelligent, honest, and with an expressed desire for a home and lasting love. Nelldean, a trusted judge of character, had extolled his virtues for weeks. Choosing her words carefully, Penny said, "If *we* — you and I — are to be together . . . Belinda and Nelldean come in the package."

"Of course. Just what I've always wanted

. . . a family," he said, and reaching out, he took her hand. "Whenever you're ready, if the answer is yes — we can resubmit these papers with both our names on it." He raised her hand to his lips and kissed it.

Penny felt the sadness lift, the loneliness that had been her companion for all these months. Maybe it was possible to love deeply, to discover a life companion with whom to share the years that lay ahead of her, to create a real home for Belinda. A warm sweetness filled her as her eyes met the ones regarding her so lovingly.

They talked quietly of immediate action and future plans. When at length he rose to leave, she walked with him into the hall. At the door he turned, and she allowed him to draw her into his arms. He cupped her chin in one hand, raised it. Looking down into her upturned face, a powerful emotion swept over him as he realized his long-held dream was coming true. He bent and kissed her softly. Her response was all he had ever imagined.

When he had somewhat regained his composure, he whispered earnestly, "I want so much for us to be together to make a home for us and Belinda. A real home is what I've always wanted, and now I know who I want to share it with me."

"How can we miss?" Penny could not resist

demanding. "That is, *if* we follow all the tenets expounded in *Handbook for Housewives: A Complete Guide to the Art of Creating a Harmonious Home, a Happy Husband, and Healthy Children.*"

She could hear him still chuckling as he walked down the path and out the gate. Standing at the door, she was filled with optimism. "Lancelot and Guinevere! Maybe there *is* a Camelot, after all — and we've found it."

The employees of Thorndike Press hope you have enjoyed this Large Print book. All our Large Print titles are designed for easy reading, and all our books are made to last. Other Thorndike Press Large Print books are available at your library, through selected bookstores, or directly from the publishers.

For more information about titles, please call:

(800) 223-1244
(800) 223-6121

To share your comments, please write:

Publisher
Thorndike Press
295 Kennedy Memorial Drive
Waterville, ME 04901